SECOND CHANCE AT LOVE

DIANNE THOMAS
OUT OF THE BLUE

BERKLEY BOOKS, NEW YORK

OUT OF THE BLUE

Copyright © 1989 by Debrah Morris and Pat Shaver

All rights reserved. No part of this publication may be reproduced or transmitted in any form or by any means, electronic or mechanical, including photocopy, recording, or any information storage and retrieval system, without permission in writing from the publisher.

Requests for permission to make copies of any part of the work should be mailed to: Permissions, Second Chance at Love, The Berkley Publishing Group, 200 Madison Avenue, New York, NY 10016.

First edition published June 1989

ISBN: 0-425-11620-4

"Second Chance at Love" and the butterfly emblem are trademarks belonging to Jove Publications, Inc. The name "BERKLEY" and the "B" logo are trademarks belonging to Berkley Publishing Corporation.

Second Chance at Love books are published by
The Berkley Publishing Group
200 Madison Avenue, New York, NY 10016

Printed in the United States of America

10 9 8 7 6 5 4 3 2 1

"I had a different game of 'doctor' in mind when I stepped on that sparkler."

April ducked under Jake's arms. "Are you saying that you actually *intended* to burn yourself?"

"Hell, no. I must have done something wrong." He sat up beside her.

"You manipulated me."

"I was desperate. And don't forget those gorgeous earlobes. They do strange things to me," Jake said with a wink. "Come on, Red. Say you'll play nurse to my doctor. Will you?" he whispered against her ear.

"I don't play games, Jake," April said. "I hate to lose."

"Red, this game is rigged." He planted his lips on hers. "There are no losers..."

Dianne Thomas

Dianne Thomas is the pseudonym of two Oklahoma women who love happy endings, other incurable romantics, and working when they should be asleep. Their ability to find humor in unlikely places provides an endless supply of inspiration and new ideas. Since they have been writing romances they've had to deal with the guilt of having a career which seems more like fun than work. Between them they have two workaholic husbands, six active children, three dogs, and several unmade beds.

Other Second Chance at Love books by
Dianne Thomas

HEAVEN CAN WAIT #364
OVERNIGHT SENSATION #460

Dear Reader:

Romance with a touch of humor is the theme this June, with two heartwarming stories by two of Second Chance at Love's most-loved veteran authors. From Dianne Thomas, the author of *Overnight Sensation* (#460), comes *Out of the Blue* (#464), the story of a mistyped basketball player with a more-than-passing interest in the mother of his irrepressible daughter's pen pal. And from Carole Buck, who most recently brought us *Simply Magic* (#459), is *Love and Laughter* (#465), starring a somewhat unconventional, though adorable, heroine . . .

April Conway and her daughter, Staci, have come to town to start a new life, far from constant reminders of the past. A bit wary but determined nonetheless, April finds herself challenged by independence as soon as she arrives at their destination. Car, clothes, and money stolen, April and Staci are stranded at the local police station. With Staci's pen pal as their only contact, they're left to the mercy of her father, Jake the Rake. Jake is an all-star athlete, a notorious womanizer, and April's last resort in more ways than one. As soon as Jake meets April, he knows his luck is turning for the better. All he's got to do is prove to his reluctant houseguest that he's just a good guy, a devoted father, and the man of her dreams. But just as Jake convinces April to envision a future in which they are together, he goes one step too far, endangering the love he treasures. *Out of the Blue* (#464) by Dianne Thomas is one not to miss.

Kelsey Howard is a clown. No kidding. She's always been one to look on the bright side. Her good nature is contagious and her optimism is unrelenting. And, even though Kelsey has just thrown a pie in his face, Elias Fletcher, genius extraordinaire, senses how much she has to offer. It's glorious luck, Elias thinks, that they should be thrown together. Kelsey has never believed more in fate than when Elias, to his own surprise, follows up on their mutual attraction. And while Elias is caught up in the pleasures of Kelsey's vibrancy and spontaneity, tendencies so unlike his own, Kelsey is pulling back. The more she falls for him, the more Kelsey fears the differences that loom. Because what Elias doesn't know is that her clowning around is partially a cover for something she's never been able to laugh about . . . *Love and Laughter* (#465) is proof that not only do opposites attract, they do so with some very highly charged results.

Also from The Berkley Publishing Group this month is *Someone in the House* by *New York Times* bestselling author Barbara Michaels, whom Mary Higgins Clark praises as a "consummate storyteller." Anne and Kevin had planned to spend their vacation writing a book at a summer retreat. But something lures them away from their work . . . something elusive, powerful, and unreal. A ghostly chilling presence that threatens more than their work . . . *Wildfire* tells the story of Serena Bain. The Yankees killed her sweetheart, imprisoned her brother, and drove her from her home. Now Serena boldly faces the future as the wagon trains roll out. Ahead are countless dangers. But all the perils in the world won't change her bitter resentment of the darkly handsome Yankee wagon master, Josh Quade. Pride and fate keep them apart. Until they meet again one night, in the soft, secret darkness . . .

Private Relations from Diane Chamberlain is a novel of love and friendship. Divorced and lonely, Kit Sheridan needed a way to revitalize her life. When word comes that her old college crowd has rented a beach house for the summer, Kit packs her bags and returns East to find refuge from her shattered dreams. The soothing rhythm of the ocean and the caring words of her friends start Kit on the road toward self-sufficiency. But it's the arrival of Cole Perelle that truly turns Kit back toward life. Within hours of meeting him, Kit finds herself telling Cole things she's never told anyone. They share everything: hopes and fears, triumphs and disappointments. There are no secrets between them. Except one: the secret which could ruin Cole's six-year relationship and destroy their friendship forever. Best friends, Kit and Cole are also in love with each other . . .

Until next month, happy reading!

Hillary Cige

Hillary Cige, Editor
SECOND CHANCE AT LOVE
The Berkley Publishing Group
200 Madison Avenue
New York, NY 10016

CHAPTER ONE

ONLY TWO DAYS off the farm and April Conway had stepped in a big one. She hated to entertain the thought so early, but maybe her in-laws were right. Maybe she wasn't qualified to take charge of her destiny after all.

Her impetuous, headlong bid for independence was supposed to lead to a bright new future for herself and her daughter. Instead it had led to this sneak preview of the seamy side of life. She surveyed the busy police station with mounting alarm and realized, for the first time, that she'd only ever seen the inside of one on television.

Whirring fans supplemented the overworked air conditioners and stirred the air, which smelled of industrial-strength cleaner. Phones rang and typewriters clacked as officers took calls and filled out reports, but mostly there were a lot of people talking at once. A detained drunk leered at April and she clasped Staci's hand a little tighter.

"...so, Mrs. Conway," the desk sergeant was saying, "we've filed your report and you're through here until something turns up. Be assured that we'll do everything we can to locate your property."

"Thank you, Sergeant Sandusky." There was a midwestern edge to April's words that contrasted sharply with the cop's soft drawl.

"If we pick up any suspects, you'll have to come down to the lineup."

"Right." The reality of the situation was slow to penetrate April's numbed brain. She hoped the sergeant would understand and forgive her lack of decisiveness. It wasn't every day that she was involved in a robbery, and she'd never been a victim before.

A dispassionate fate had placed her in the wrong convenience store at precisely the wrong moment. Her own stupidity had placed her car, with keys still in the ignition, smack dab in the thieves' getaway path.

While she and Staci and the store clerk lay sprawled on the floor with their lives passing before them, two young hoodlums had emptied the cash drawer and beer box. April's first thought had been for Staci's safety, but close behind that was the smug feeling that she'd outsmarted the robbers by tucking her purse—containing all her traveler's checks, credit cards, and cash—under the seat of the car before going inside the store to pay for gas and soft drinks.

That smugness was short-lived. While the clerk called the police, April stared outside at the empty spot where she'd parked her two-year-old Bronco.

"Mrs. Conway?" Sergeant Sandusky cleared his throat and pushed a clipboard toward her across his cluttered desk. "Just sign here, and put your address and telephone number down so we can get in touch with you."

April's thoughts had left the police station; returning now, she blinked up at the sergeant. She had to get a grip on herself. She had to think about what she was going to do. More important, she had to say something intelligent.

"What?"

"Sign here."

She reached for the pen and panicked. Did she dare tell him she didn't have an address, much less a telephone number? Would he feel obliged to enforce whatever laws the city had against vagrancy? She'd come here with the intention of becoming a useful citizen, but she and Staci had arrived exactly fifteen minutes prior to being relieved of their worldly possessions. The apartment she'd leased wouldn't be ready for two more weeks, and she'd planned to stay in a motel until then. April signed her name and scrawled "to be determined" on the address line.

"You can use this phone to call somebody to come get you."

Easy for him to say. "That'll be a bit tricky since I don't know anyone in Jacksonville. Nor do I know anyone in Florida. In fact, I don't know anyone on the entire eastern seaboard." April was dangerously close to losing control and the realization worried her.

Staci yanked on her hand and whispered, "I know someone," but April ignored her. The adrenaline that had prevented her from collapsing in fright during the robbery had ebbed. The shaky uncertainty that had replaced it was slowly being usurped by an outraged sense of justice.

"What kind of town is this, anyway?" she asked rhetorically as her hands flew up in a hopeless gesture. "Welcome to Jacksonville; this is a stickup! Why me?"

Experience had given Sergeant Sandusky a more objective outlook. "I'm sorry, Mrs. Conway, but these things happen. You and your daughter can stay here until you work something out, but you'll have to make other arrangements soon. This is no place for a child."

April gave him her "no-kidding" look as a door swung open and a uniformed policeman pushed a scruffy-looking young man down in a nearby chair. The officer clutched the front of the kid's shirt and, looking him dead in the eye, warned, "Don't move while I'm gone, punk. Don't even breathe."

April groaned. She'd wanted to see the world beyond her in-laws' three hundred acres. However, this was not the part she'd had in mind. "I'm not sure what arrangements I can make, officer." She dug into the pocket of her white jeans and pulled out a handful of change. Counting it, she announced, "I have exactly eighty-three cents. Do you know of a really cut-rate motel within walking distance?"

Sergeant Sandusky shook his head. "Don't you know anybody who can wire you money?"

Staci piped up, "Grampa and Gramma would send some, Mom."

That was true. They'd send enough for two one-way tickets back to Iowa and take perverse pleasure in pointing out that they'd told her so. April refused to go back with her tail tucked between her legs, and her firm "No!" left no room for discussion.

"There's a reasonably clean shelter for the homeless downtown," the sergeant suggested. "They're pretty crowded but they might have a couple of cots for the night."

A shelter for the homeless? April's spirits sank even lower. Had she left the suffocating security of the past two years for such an uncertain future? The Conways had accused her of being selfish. Was it possible that she had been thinking only of herself? Was she still? Maybe the whole idea of establishing a life of her own had been a big mistake and she was just too proud or too dumb to admit it.

Her decision to leave Strawberry Point had been met with disbelief by everyone but her best friend, who'd told her to "go for it." Suze had expressed belief in her. Everyone else had told her it was foolish for a widow with a young child to take risks when she had a perfectly good home with her late husband's parents.

That was why she couldn't call anyone for help. She didn't want to give any of them the satisfaction. She couldn't call Suze because she didn't want her friend to know she had made such a mess of things so soon.

"Define reasonably clean," Staci commanded with all the aplomb an eleven-year-old could muster when faced with the possibility of sleeping on a cot in a room full of strangers.

"No, don't." April stood up straighter and her five feet seven inches seemed more imposing. She brushed back several tendrils of long auburn hair that had escaped her hot-pink headband and spoke with more assurance than she felt.

"This situation is temporary. I'll admit that at the moment we are technically destitute. But in the morning, I'll simply call my bank back home and have it forward money to a new account. Then we'll rent a car, find a motel room, buy some clothes, and pretend this was all a bad dream." April was satisfied. It sounded like a really good plan.

"Can't," intoned Staci.

Distracted, April turned to her daughter. "And why can't we?"

"Because tomorrow's Saturday."

April sighed. "And we can't get a wire transfer on Saturday." Any more setbacks and she might not be able to contain all the screams building up inside her. But then, venting her true feelings would ensure her of a nice, comfortable place to sleep—at the state's expense in a padded cell somewhere. "Okay." She waved dismissively. "We can't do that, so we'll just... we'll just... sit on that bench until Monday."

"Can't," said the sergeant.

"And why not, pray tell?" April muttered through clenched teeth.

"It's against regulations, and besides, Monday's the Fourth of July. All the banks are closed."

Staci yanked on April's hand again. "I know someone here, Mom."

April knew what her daughter was about to suggest. "Having a pen pal isn't the same as knowing someone. We've never met the Keegans and we can't call total strangers."

"Molly and I have been writing to each other for three years. That should count for something," Staci said indignantly.

Sergeant Sandusky looked at the clock and his expression said he'd wasted enough time on them already. "If there's any chance at all that you can get help, Mrs. Conway, I'd suggest you make the call."

April wavered, knowing for the first time what it meant to be caught between the devil and the deep blue sea. She had no wish to cast her daughter and herself into the murky waters of public charity, nor did she want to ask help of Jake "The Rake" Keegan, a man whose publicized exploits were devilish indeed.

You're in charge now, she told herself. Be decisive. What will it be, a public shelter or Jake the Rake? He was a star basketball jock with a dubious reputation, and his nickname was attributed to his conquests off the court as well as on. He wasn't exactly the Good Samaritan type. If the media were to be believed, he had long since gained professional-playboy status.

"I vote we call the Keegans," Staci put in.

"No voting," April said firmly, suddenly regretting the democratic way she'd brought up her daughter. She glanced at the sergeant, who was trying not to eavesdrop.

"You wouldn't be talking about Jake Keegan, would you?"

"Yes," Staci confirmed. "Do you know him?"

"Sure. Everybody in Jacksonville knows Jake the Rake. Of course I haven't met him in person, but I never miss one of the Jags' home games. They won the playoffs this year and helped me win a fifty-dollar bet." He slid the phone toward April. "You know his home number?"

"I do," squealed Staci. She unzipped the small fuschia handbag strapped to her belt, fished out a notebook and handed it to Sandusky. The sergeant started dialing before April could protest.

"Wait just a darn minute. I don't know this Keegan guy, and I certainly don't want to ask him for help."

"Here you go, Mrs. Conway." A beaming Sergeant Sandusky thrust the phone into her hand. "It's ringing."

"A little lower, honey. Ah, that's good." Jake Keegan's long, athletic frame was stretched on a pool-side chaise longue and a girl whose name he didn't remember was rubbing lotion on his already tanned back.

Some of his friends had thought to cheer him up by throwing him a surprise party; he always got so depressed on his birthday. So far, it wasn't working, but if the nimble-fingered blonde kept up the good work, he might come around yet.

Birthdays were a pain in the neck, and while there'd been a certain sense of accomplishment in attaining the first twenty-one, he'd felt the pressure of these past few years. If he kept having birthdays, sooner or later people would expect him to act like a grown-up.

Birthdays were supposed to be an excuse to eat cake and act stupid, but for Jake, they were a time to take stock of his life. Each year he felt obliged to examine where he'd been and where he was going. Such evaluations invariably made him grouchy, but he persisted because he was a goal-setter. Ever since he was a kid, once he decided what he wanted, he didn't let up until he got it.

He'd ended the NBA season by leading his team to a national title and in so doing, had attained a very important goal. His career in pro basketball was nearing its natural conclusion and he'd planned all year to go out big. Very big. He didn't want to wait until age and injuries forced him out of the game. He wanted to go out in a blaze of glory, and his recent success made retirement a distinct possibility.

Now he had the World Championship ring, the trophy, the applause, *and* the glory. Just when he was feeling particularly full of himself, this damned birthday had come up. Turning thirty-three reminded him that he still didn't have anyone special to share his life with.

He'd never worried about such things before, and now he wondered if the surge of "settle-down" hormones was part of the same aging process as were his sudden inability to party all night and his growing disinterest in the inhabitants of "bimbo limbo." Whatever it was, he'd been feeling a lonesome lack for some time now.

"How're you doing, my man?"

Jake turned over and squinted up at his best friend and teammate, Chaz Morton. He glanced pointedly at the blonde, who resumed her ministrations on his smooth chest.

"I'm trying to bear up."

The lanky black man grinned at the girl. "Why don't you take a dip and cool off? Me and my friend have got some talking to do." She moved away and Chaz whistled under his breath.

"You realize, of course," Jake pointed out, "that some foreign countries issue stamps larger than that bikini she's wearing."

"Yeah, but they don't look as good."

"Have you seen Molly lately?"

"She's in the house with Ivy." Chaz settled down in a nearby chair. "Those two make a pair," he said of his wife and Jake's daughter. "Ivy wants to be a mother, and Molly needs one."

"Don't remind me." Jake was acutely aware that his twelve-year-old daughter was growing up without a stable feminine influence. His sister, Mary Margaret, was a big help, but with five kids of her own, she didn't have time to practice much discipline. Instead, she relied on crowd control, and Molly sometimes got lost in the shuffle.

Molly had insisted he turn down Mags's invitation to have dinner with her family in St. Augustine. "Be honest, Pops. Dinner with good old Aunt Mags the Nag and Uncle Fred the Walking Dead and their five kids can't really be your idea of a fun way to spend your birthday. What that woman can do to an unsuspecting corn-beef-and-cabbage should be against the law."

She'd been teasing, but he'd felt obliged to chide her, even though she was right; his sister and brother-in-law were a bit dull around the edges.

"If it weren't for Mary Margaret, you never would've survived potty training, so show some respect. Fred and Mags have been good to both of us, and they're wonderful people."

"I know, Pops," she had agreed. "But you've been an old grump lately, and the play-offs took a lot out of you. You need to meet some nice lady—and I emphasize the word lady—settle down, and get married. I won't be around forever, you know."

He had smiled down at his daughter who thought she was his mother, and realized that she needed someone special in her life as much as he did. "Why do you insist on matchmaking?"

Her impish grin had been a reflection of his own. "It's a dirty job, but somebody has to do it."

"Hey." Chaz waved a hand before Jake's face as if to rouse him from a reverie. Always Molly's willing accomplice, he said, "It's time for our bimonthly when-are-you-going-to-settle-down-and-get-married discussion."

Jake propped his hands behind his head and closed his eyes behind dark glasses. "Et tu, Brutus?" At Chaz's puzzled look, he explained. "Molly and I had the same discussion earlier today."

"So what are you waiting for, man?"

"I guess I haven't met the right woman."

Slipping effortlessly into a Columbo impersonation, Chaz scrunched up one side of his face and muttered, "Correct me if I'm wrong, but as I recall, you have to do what is commonly known as beatin' 'em off with a stick."

Jake laughed. No one could stay glum around Chaz; that was one reason they'd been friends for ten years. "I don't meet the *right* kind of women. Sports groupies aren't spouse material and regular women don't take me seriously."

"Why should they, man? You've never given them any indication that you have a serious side."

"I know. It's easier to play the part of a fun-loving jock with a severe allergy to commitment. It fits the image, and the fans don't want their heroes to display too much sensitivity."

"Maybe, but women do. Don't you read *Cosmo*? Ivy says there's someone in the world for everyone, even Jake the Rake. The thing is, you gotta look in the right places. Serious ladies tend to get put off by rabid clusters of semi-attached females."

"Where do you suggest I meet one of these serious ladies?"

His friend shrugged. "I found mine in the produce department. I can't tell you where to look, but you sure can't sit around here waiting for her to come to you. Ms. Right is not going to call you up and say, 'Here I am, Mister Sports Hero. Come and get me.'" This time he sounded suspiciously like Butterfly McQueen.

April waited with trepidation through eight rings. When she was about to hang up, a soft-sounding female voice answered. "May I speak to Jake Keegan, please?" April asked meekly.

"Turn down that music, will you?" the woman commanded. "I can't hear a thing. Excuse me, what did you say?"

"Jake Keegan. Is he there?" A hush fell over the station when April mentioned the name, and she looked up. Policemen and perpetrators alike were hanging on to her every word. A flurry of "What about them Jags?" drifted around the room.

April waited for the woman's answer. "Sure, hold on."

Across town, Molly raced out of the house and called to

the assembly in general, "Put a lid on the hedonism, guys. There's a minor among you." She tossed Jake a cordless phone. "It's for you, Pops."

Jake ran his fingers through his hair and wondered if he had made a mistake in trying to raise her alone. "Where did you get that stuff?"

She danced away. "Too much time spent in the corrupting environment of the locker room, I guess."

"Who is it?"

She shook her head and the blond ponytail that was skewed over her left ear bobbed. "I don't know, but Ivy said it was a w-o-m-a-n."

"That ought to narrow it down to a couple of million, huh?" Chaz asked the tall men and voluptuous women who were lounging around the pool.

Jake grimaced and covered his other ear to muffle the laughter greeting Chaz's remark. "Keegan. I'm sorry, but I can't hear you." By way of explanation, he added, "We're having a party here."

"How nice for you." The prudish female voice sounded disapproving and Jake waited impatiently for the woman to state her business.

April rolled her eyes when she heard a high-pitched voice in the background remind him that it was his turn to rub lotion on her. How lucky. She'd caught the party animal in its natural habitat.

Jake clamped one hand over the mouthpiece and yelled at a couple of nubile water-fighters who'd splashed him. "Give me a break, girls. I'm on the phone here."

Girls? As in plural? Just how decadent was the famous debauchee? Poor little Molly. April wanted to hang up, but everyone in the station, including Staci and Sergeant Sandusky, was waiting expectantly. Part of her resisted asking someone like Keegan for aid, but she'd have to go through with it.

"We've never met, but my name is April Conway."

"Can I help you with something?" As far as Jake could tell, there wasn't much point to the conversation.

"I'm Staci Conway's mother. Our daughters are pen pals."

Of course. Jake knew of the Conways. Molly's long-distance friendship with Staci was very important to her, and she had been thrilled when she'd learned that the family was moving to Jacksonville. He motioned to his daughter to join him; maybe Staci wanted to talk to her.

Prompted by Sergeant Sandusky, April blurted, "We just arrived today, and earlier this evening we were involved in a robbery in which my car and all my money were stolen. We're stranded at the police station, and since we don't know a soul in town, I didn't know who else to call."

April stopped momentarily to rid her voice of its edge of desperation. "Through no fault of my own, I've been reduced to vagrant status, and unless you can come get us, we'll have to stay in a public shelter until the banks open on Tuesday."

Once more Jake ran a hand through his rich brown hair. The lady told quite a story, and it was much too pitiful to be anyone's idea of a joke. He had no idea what he was supposed to do with them once he picked them up, but he couldn't, in good conscience, abandon a woman and her little girl to fate. They were fresh off the farm and no doubt incapable of dealing with the problems encountered in a big city.

With no thought to the ironic coincidence of April Conway's words and Chaz's, he assured her, "I'll be there as soon as I can."

With one eye on the clock and a restraining hand on Staci, April waited. She wasn't sure of what she'd say to Keegan when he arrived, but she'd start with "thank you" and go from there. Once she explained everything, he might be willing to lend her some money for the weekend.

She'd have no trouble repaying him—her account back

home contained the benefits from all three of Caleb's life-insurance policies. Her husband had insisted on carrying a lot of insurance, claiming he wanted to leave her well provided for should anything happen to him. Perhaps he, too, had doubted her ability to take care of herself.

The outside doors swung open and April looked up with expectancy and dread to see if Keegan had arrived. She sighed as a policewoman herded several colorfully dressed women into the room. Their appearance and demeanor left little doubt as to their occupation, and April drew Staci closer to her on the bench. The cop told the newcomers to wait for booking, and two of them sat down beside her.

April smiled at her bench mates uncertainly. One of the women was dressed all in black and had long, straight black hair that hung over her shoulders, strategically covering what the leather bikini top under her fishnet half-blouse did not. Knee-high boots hugged her legs, but there was still a foot of bare skin between boot tops and black mini-skirt.

The other had spiky pink hair and blue lightning flashes painted on both cheeks. She wore a gold-lamé halter dress that revealed a small snake tattoo on one shoulder. "Tattoo" lit a long brown cigarette and blew smoke in April's direction.

"What part of town you workin', hon?"

April stifled the gasp that rose in her throat, and before she could answer, Staci volunteered, "Mom's unemployed at the moment."

Tattoo turned to her companion and they laughed. "Unemployed? You hear that, Bootsy? I guess we are, too, huh?"

Bootsy leaned over her friend's knee and tapped April's arm. "Don't mind Nadia. She ain't as refined as you and me."

April smiled halfheartedly and turned away, convinced that the awful night would never end. She had to get Staci out of here, and if Jake the Rake was her only hope, so be it. "Staci, do you need to go to the ladies' room?" she asked encouragingly.

Staci shook her head and her red curls bounced. "I've already been."

"Hey, Sarge!" Nadia bellowed. "How come you let her go to the john and not us?"

Bootsy stood up and demanded her rights.

Sergeant Sandusky pointed a thick, menacing finger at the troublemakers. "You haven't been booked yet. Sit down and wait your turn like good little girls." When Bootsy plopped down, he returned his attention to the papers on his desk.

Staci's eyes were on the two women; she was seemingly intrigued by their outlandish clothes. "Are you two some kind of performers?"

Nadia cackled and poked Bootsy in the ribs with her elbow. "You can say that again, kid."

April squeezed Staci's hand. Her daughter had led a sheltered life and knew little of the world. Would she adjust to living in a much different environment from the one they'd left behind? One of the reasons for the move was to give Staci the cultural advantages of city life and the extracurricular activities her small country school couldn't offer. April closed her eyes, hoping again that she'd made the right decision.

When she opened them and scanned the room, her gaze caught the back view of a tall man standing in front of the sergeant's desk. He was at least six feet five, and when she realized that he was probably Keegan, her heart hurried in response. She wasn't sure of what it was about him that triggered her unexpected reaction, but she could feel his crackling vitality all the way across the room.

His brown hair, thick and streaked with blond, was in need of a trim, and April was fascinated by the way it caressed the back of his neck. He wore a white cotton T-shirt shaped with obvious, but not bulging, muscles, and his shoulders formed the top of a triangle that tapered into a lean waist. Snug stone-washed jeans rode his narrow hips and encased his long legs. He had an air of casual confidence that said he was comfortable with himself, and with a body that would make heads turn wherever he went.

Whatever it was about him, it played havoc with April's imagination and he caught her staring at him when he turned around and strode toward them. Her hand went unconsciously to her hair when she read the slogan emblazoned in scarlet across the front of his shirt. The words, "I BRAKE FOR REDHEADS," were made even more prominent by the shelf of his well-defined pectoral muscles.

April had been prepared for a face to match the physique, and she wasn't disappointed. With his dark eyes, sensual lips, and five-o'clock shadow, he surpassed handsome, but it was his secret expression that made him so riveting. When his brown eyes connected with hers, April realized his magnetism went beyond good looks. His eyes reflected intelligence and compassion, and quite against her will, a force within her surged. Her pulses quickened and she felt a breathless wonder that any man could affect her so. Beside her, Bootsy and Nadia voiced their approval of his male perfection with low whistles.

Jake recognized the Widow Conway the moment he entered the station; she and her daughter looked as out of place as flowers growing through the sidewalk. The fresh-faced woman, whose rich auburn hair fairly glowed in the bright room, was clutching the hand of a freckly-faced pixie and watching him nervously.

She had the prettiest eyes he'd ever seen, and he felt himself being drawn into their blue depths. His fingers tingled and he found himself caught by the thought of stroking her shiny hair and touching her pale skin. He felt an attraction so unique, so strong, that he shivered.

He stopped in front of the group on the bench and extended his hand to the child. "Hi, I'm Jake. You must be Staci."

Staci grabbed his hand in both of hers. "I'm so glad to see you, Mr. Keegan. Thanks for coming."

"No problem. And call me Jake." Scrutinizing the three women seated beside her, he asked with a grin, "Tell me, Staci, which one of these lovely ladies is your mother?"

CHAPTER TWO

JUST THEN MOLLY skidded around the corner, her ponytail swinging. "Staci! You're here! You're finally here," she squealed. The girls embraced and chattered, totally uninhibited by either the circumstances or their surroundings.

The flush that had risen in April's cheeks at Keegan's amused question was fading, but her body was still diffused with warmth. She was ready with righteous indignation, but when she saw his twinkling eyes, she knew he was teasing and let it go.

"Thank you for coming." She rose and shook Jake's hand. He held it a beat longer than good manners dictated, and a totally inappropriate tingle skittered along her nerves. Irritated by her reaction, she quickly slipped her hand from his. "I'm sorry we had to meet under such unlikely circumstances, Mr. Keegan."

He looked at her with an expression that made her wonder what he was thinking. "I'm just glad we met."

His directness made April uneasy, and she had second thoughts about placing herself in his hands. Even figuratively. "I don't know how I'll ever repay you for this."

"Don't worry." His deep voice was both soothing and disconcerting. "Between us, we'll think of something." He put his arm around her shoulders in a familiar, brotherly way and the four of them stepped out into the balmy night air.

After determining that no one had yet had dinner, Jake stopped at his favorite pizzeria on the way home. His friends had long since left and the house was quiet when they arrived. He was glad. He wanted to get acquainted with the lady without anyone else's curious, well-meaning meddling. He was intrigued by the fatefulness of the situation, and a secretive little smile played about his lips. And Chaz had said he shouldn't wait around for Ms. Right to call him.

April was uncomfortable eating pizza in a strange man's kitchen, and her uneasiness showed. But since that stranger had just rescued Staci and her from spending the night in a shelter and had offered the carry-out dinner, the least she could do was to be grateful.

"Thank you again, Mr. Keegan," she said sincerely.

"Call me Jake. I hope you won't let what happened today give you a bad impression of Floridians. Our armed-robber-per-capita ratio is no higher than elsewhere." He bit into a wedge of pizza, and the hot cheese stretched into a long string that he disposed of with finesse.

April watched in fascination as his tongue stroked a drop of sauce from his lips, and almost forgot to reply. "Not at all. I like what I've seen so far." Too late she realized how flirtatious the remark sounded and averted her eyes. Something about Jake Keegan made it impossible to ignore the fact that he was an uncommonly large and unfairly attractive male animal.

"Thank you." Jake accepted the compliment for Florida in general or for himself, whichever she'd had in mind.

April stared at him, certain she'd never encountered anyone with so much self-confidence. Not that it wasn't completely justified. Even if she hadn't known he was a professional athlete, she would have guessed it. His muscles were well-defined under his ridiculous T-shirt and the fluidity of his movements bespoke arduous training. Here was a man who would definitely look good in sweaty gym clothes.

Despite his flamboyant reputation, Jake had said or done nothing untoward since they'd arrived at his home. In fact, he had been a perfect host, charming and genial in every way. He'd listened attentively as April described the robbery, and his concern had seemed genuine.

But his sensuous smiles and lazy, measuring glances reminded her that he wasn't known as Jake the Rake for nothing. They told her that his was a powerful and barely leashed sexuality, one that made her intensely aware of her own longings. It had taken two years of widowhood to put her unwanted yearnings in their place, and she didn't need a man like Jake Keegan to remind her of their existence. Just being here was somehow dangerous, and she wished belatedly that she had taken her chances in the shelter.

Roaches and lack of privacy she could handle. Taut muscles and smoldering glances were beyond her realm of experience. After being widowed, she had made a few attempts at dating, but not since Caleb had she felt so much frightening man-woman awareness. She was more threatened than a thirty-year-old woman who'd sworn she could take care of herself should be. Not so much by his interest in her, which didn't mean much coming from a man like Keegan, but by the intensity of her response. Was she so hungry for male attention that she could be taken in by a notorious womanizer? She was uncomfortable under his scrutiny, but tried to eat her pizza. Maybe the mere act of chewing would preclude further small talk until she mustered up the resources required to deal with him.

Unlike her daughter, April did not immediately feel at ease in the Keegan home. She had certain expectations of how a person with more money than taste should decorate, and this wasn't it. The striking Tudor, located in the exclusive Deerfield area, was as imposing as its owner, whose magnetic presence filled and overflowed the spacious and tastefully decorated rooms.

Nor did she find the comfort in Jake's company that Staci found in Molly's. The two girls had insisted on taking their pizza upstairs to Molly's room so they could "talk and stuff," functions adolescent girls were unable to perform in the presence of adults.

"I think the girls really hit it off," Jake offered, hoping to move on to new conversational territory. They'd already discussed the robbery, the weather, and schools. He wanted to know more about this woman who'd appeared so unexpectedly in his life.

"Yes, they did. I'm still amazed that Staci has taken the robbery so casually. She's treated the whole thing as some kind of big adventure. I believe her word for it was 'crucial.'"

April was worried about the effect the event might have on her daughter, who still suffered an occasional nightmare over her father's tragic death. Staci had been one of the reasons she had fought so hard to leave Iowa. They both needed a life where the past wasn't so much a part of the future.

"Children are more resilient than we adults give them credit for," Jake observed. "Did you find it a big adventure?"

"I was terrified. My first concern was for Staci's safety, but I was also worried that the news would somehow get back to Strawberry Point. If it did, I'd be forced to admit my incompetence."

He looked at her curiously, and she noticed the faint lines about his mouth and eyes that muted his handsome face with strength. "No one could hold you responsible. It was simply a case of being in the wrong place at the wrong time."

"I know that, and you know that. But Staci's grandparents wouldn't see it that way. I'd be accused of gross negligence for allowing her to get involved in a crime. In their eyes, I'd be as guilty as if I'd robbed that store myself." April drew a sharp breath, dismayed that she'd spoken her feelings aloud. Normally she wasn't such a blabbermouth.

Jake grinned and a tiny dimple appeared near the corner of his mouth. "If they give you any trouble, I'll be happy to vouch for you."

The warmth of that smile touched a need in April that she had forgotten was there, and she returned it. "I think that finally meeting Molly was more important to Staci than a mere garden-variety holdup." Her words were light, belying her mounting anxiety over a very real problem. There had been no discussion of arrangements and she had no idea of what she would do once the evening's hospitality was over.

She had no money, and no chance of getting any until after the holiday. She didn't want to ask Jake for a loan, and more than that, she simply would not call the Conways for help. They would enjoy pointing out that her plans had been doomed from the beginning and demand she come back.

"Staci will be good for Molly." Jake rose and began clearing away the remains of their impromptu dinner. It disturbed April that he looked as comfortable with a dishcloth in his hand as he would a basketball. He chuckled wryly. "Sometimes I worry that she's growing up too fast. Our lifestyle isn't conducive to prolonged childhood."

April could well imagine. How inconvenient he must find traveling in the fast lane with the ballast of a child slowing him down. One glance at the slogan on his shirt reminded her of the reputation that seemed in contrast to the man. If he braked for redheads, what did he do for blondes and brunettes?

Jake saw the direction her eyes had taken and he pinched up the front of his shirt. "I should probably explain this."

"Not at all. Even though I don't share it, I understand

the compulsion some people have to advertise their modus vivendi."

Jake's soft laughter wrapped around her like mink. "Normally I don't need to advertise. I just got this today and grabbed it when I was getting dressed to come down to the station." When she looked skeptical, he added, "It was a birthday gift from someone who knows me all too well." He didn't tell her that Chaz had given it to him as a joke because of his preference for blondes. He watched April with growing interest and wondered why he'd never noticed auburn hair before.

April felt a stab of unreasonable envy that someone, probably a red-haired beauty, knew him better than she. "Did my call interrupt your birthday party?" She felt chastened; she'd had visions of an orgy when she had talked to him on the phone. Everyone was entitled to a birthday party.

"No problem. Thanks to you, it's been one of the most memorable birthdays I've ever had."

She blushed and wished he'd stop saying things like that. No doubt he was a practiced flatterer, one of those men who seem to know instinctively what a woman needs and how to effortlessly give it to her. Was his penchant for women responsible for the absence of Molly's mother?

Shortly after Caleb's death, Molly had written Staci a heartfelt sympathy letter containing the line, "I know it seems tough right now, but believe me, you can survive with only one parent." Staci had shared the letter with April, and at the time, April had found the words a bit cynical coming from a ten-year-old. Molly had made no other reference, before or after, to her mother, and April had often wondered about the stability of the child's life.

Now that she had met Molly, who seemed well-adjusted but wise beyond her years, she understood the spirit in which the remark had been made. It was simply an earnest attempt at reassurance by a child who had already lost a parent. Maybe Molly had a right to be cynical. According to Staci, she stayed with her aunt and uncle while Jake traveled, and April suspected that the girl had learned to survive with no parent at all.

"Despite our less-than-auspicious beginning, I think life here will be good for Staci, too. She took her father's death very hard."

Jake poured coffee into two large mugs and set one of them on the table in front of April before offering her sugar and cream. "I know," he admitted. "Molly told me all about it." He didn't know how to talk to a widow. That status automatically made April different from all the career women and divorcées he knew, who were single by choice.

April looked up in surprise, her sense of vulnerability increased by the knowledge that this man obviously knew a lot more about her than she knew about him. "She did?" Her daughter's acceptance of Caleb's death had been slow in coming. Evidently she'd used her letters to Molly as a catharsis, and April was relieved to know that she'd had such an outlet.

"Yes. Staci really poured her heart out in the letters she wrote after her father's death. Molly had never experienced death at first or even second hand, and she came to me for help in dealing with it."

"And did you advise her on what to write Staci?" It was disturbing that Jake had already had some input into their lives; that without her knowledge, a seed of familiarity had been planted.

"No," he said thoughtfully. "I answered Molly's questions but I told her that only she would know how to comfort her friend. She seemed satisfied with that."

So was April.

They sipped their coffee for a few moments longer, and Jake wondered why he wasn't irritated by having to bail a total stranger out of a mess. His party had been disrupted, and now it appeared that his life, for the next few days at least, would be disrupted as well. He was attracted by

April's milkmaid prettiness and found her guileless, upfront manner charming, but those things didn't really explain his feelings.

There were any number of people he could have assigned to take care of the matter. So why hadn't he? Maybe it had been April's voice that had compelled him to act. She'd sounded as though she expected indifference from him. More likely it was Molly's friendship with Staci. Jake paused in his reflections. He didn't practice self-deception, nor was he accustomed to having his brain override his hormones when it came to women. But this woman was different, and for once he was astute enough to recognize it.

April wasn't very accomplished at hiding her thoughts, and Jake felt like a voyeur every time he watched a thought or a feeling flicker across her face. Her inherent honesty and gentleness appealed to him. Although there was undoubtedly a strong woman beneath that tender exterior, she made him feel like a knight who had just rescued an innocent damsel. A damsel who could have assuredly slain the dragon herself if given enough time.

Since April seemed unwilling to discuss her deceased husband, he changed the subject. "Molly tells me you're planning to open a restaurant here. Why Jacksonville? Don't you have restaurants in Wisconsin?"

"Iowa," April corrected automatically. "I have several reasons for migrating south, escape from the dreadful winters for one. Also, I've been here before, a long time ago, and I like the area." Her other reasons were more valid but too personal to discuss with this charming stranger. She could hardly tell him that she had fallen in love with the place on her honeymoon, or that it was the only place where she'd ever truly had Caleb to herself. Nor could she admit that she'd never muster the courage to assert herself in a town where she'd always been known as "Caleb's little woman."

Jake sensed the weather wasn't all she was trying to

escape. "Are you running from a ghost by any chance?" he asked bluntly.

The unexpected question startled April. In Strawberry Point, everyone knew everyone else's business, but there was an unspoken protocol that governed the amount of prying a decent person could do. No one she knew would dream of asking a casual acquaintance such a question. She looked at him levelly before deciding to dignify it with an answer. "Perhaps."

She didn't elaborate, and Jake was wise enough to drop what was obviously a painful subject. He knew she'd lost her husband two years ago. Was that a sufficiently long mourning period? Or hadn't she gotten over the loss at all?

Jake wasn't sure he wanted to compete with a dead husband who'd been, according to his daughter, "the greatest guy in the world," a man so noble and heroic in spirit that he'd died while saving the lives of others.

Given her obvious disapproval of himself and his lifestyle, persuading the widow of such a man to look beyond Jake the Rake's public image might be difficult. But then again, the competitive drive was strong within him and he was intrigued enough by her to face the challenge she presented. His reputation hadn't been a problem during the years in which he had worked so assiduously to earn it. It had attracted a lot of women who were as shallow and insincere as they thought he was.

But April was neither shallow or insincere. She was obviously a sensible exception to the self-centered rule, and he sensed that winning her trust would be worth the effort. For the first time in his life, he was tempted to justify himself, and he wondered irritably if it was due to those "settle-down" hormones again or to April's cool distance that needled him.

Recalling the conversation he'd had earlier with Chaz, it occurred to Jake that perhaps fate was playing a nasty little joke on him. He didn't know much about the statistical probability that a woman like April would show up when he most needed to meet her. But he knew that it was time to shuck off the facade he had hidden behind for so long. It was time for the real Jake Keegan to stand up.

There were big problems to overcome if he was going to attract her serious attention, but one thing was on his side! He had what could be called a captive audience. The woman had no clothes, no car, and no money. He didn't want her to think she was at his mercy, but when you got right down to it, she was.

He had until Tuesday to decide if his interest was genuine or simply a case of wanting something he couldn't have. In order to do that, he'd need to know more about her so he could begin plotting his strategy.

"What are your plans, once you get settled?" he asked casually.

April had the feeling that he was talking about personal plans, not professional ones, and she shifted restlessly in her chair. Why did he insist on small talk when there were some really big issues to settle? Like where she was going to sleep, for example. "They're pretty unformed right now, but I've always been interested in the restaurant business."

"What a coincidence. Me, too."

April checked his expression to see if he was sincere. It appeared he was. Someone in his position could do anything he wanted to do, while making this start had been a difficult move for her. "I've never had the nerve to do anything about it until now. Why are you smiling?"

"Because you don't strike me as a woman who lacks courage."

"You don't know me very well." She raised her cup and the steam made her blink.

"A situation I plan to correct," he said disarmingly. He looked at her steadily and the double meaning of his gaze became as obvious as that of the word "know."

April gulped and the hot coffee seared her throat. She was expected to say something, but surely suffering first-degree burns of the esophagus relieved her of that obligation.

Jake fought the temptation to offer her ice water; it would squelch the heat he felt growing between them. Aware of her discomposure, he realized he had a chance after all. "What kind of restaurant?"

She glanced at him, her frustration clear. Sometime during the evening, Jake had failed her by not being the dumb macho jerk she'd expected. Worse, he showed every sign of being an astute, witty, and sensitive human being. She had been prepared to dislike him and all he stood for, but she'd lost control of her responses halfway through the pizza.

"I want a place with a friendly neighborhood ambience. Good food, a well-stocked bar, maybe a piano and a singer on weekends. A place where people can eat and talk and be entertained."

Her enthusiasm added a beguiling sparkle to her eyes, and Jake felt the pull more fiercely than ever. "Sounds good. But do you have any idea of how competitive the restaurant business is here? Do you have any experience?"

"Not exactly in restaurants. I do have experience in food service. I was in charge of planning and overseeing the school lunch program for the three elementary schools in our district back home." April was proud of the fact that she had won the battle to make the menus more nutritious and more appealing to the children, but she knew that her accomplishment must sound like pretty small potatoes to Jake.

The little dimple appeared beside the corner of his mouth as he teased, "Will that be your specialty? With all the craze for nostalgia, you might find a yuppie audience for school-cafeteria cuisine."

She grinned back at him and took up the joke. "I can see the menu now. Salisbury steak and fluffy whipped potatoes, wacky cake and spiced applesauce, among other tasty treats."

"Don't forget the cast-iron meatloaf and the tuna surprise, two of my perennial favorites." They laughed, and Jake was struck by the way laughter transformed her. Had he thought her pretty? Damn, she was beautiful. "Seriously, what's your gimmick?"

"Gimmick?" April wondered what he was referring to.

"You know, your something special."

"If I provide good food value for the dollar and excellent service, why do I need a gimmick?"

This time his smile was indulgent. "Just to get the public's attention. You'll be competing against places that aren't above using 'Wet T-shirt Night' to draw a crowd."

"I won't be after the singles' trade," she defended. "I want a place where women can go alone and not worry about being hit on. Where men can gather and discuss business without the distraction of skimpily clad waitresses. Mine won't be a romantic first-date place, but a cozy twenty-first-anniversary place."

Jake shook his head skeptically. "You'll still need a gimmick."

"I'm a long way from worrying about that. I have to find a suitable location, get financing, obtain all the licenses, come up with a menu, contact vendors, and hire a staff. Then I'll worry about gimmicks."

Obviously she'd done her homework, so Jake simply wished her luck. He didn't add that she would need it if she were to carve a place for herself in such a cut-throat business.

The girls came bounding into the kitchen to add their pizza box to the detritus that had already been cleared away.

"Molly's been showing me around, Mom." Staci's excitement punctuated her words. "Boy, is this a cool house or what?"

April rejoiced in the light shining from her daughter's eyes; it had been dimmed for too long. "It certainly is." She turned back to Jake, suddenly, inexplicably, happy to be where she was. "You really do have a lovely home."

Before he could respond, Molly quipped, "Not what you'd expect old Jake the Rake to go for, huh? No tiger prints, no mirrored ceilings, no initials set in wrought iron." She hugged her father and plopped onto his knee. "Poor Pops," she cooed. "He just ain't what he's cracked up to be."

Jake's sigh was long-suffering, the hug he gave his daughter loving. "Darling Molly, the bane of my existence, the joy of my life. I have no one but myself to blame for the way she's turned out." His tone left no doubt that he was pleased with the result, and Molly planted a big kiss on his cheek.

April wondered if the child were psychic. If Molly hadn't read her earlier thoughts, what explanation could there be for those remarks? Turning to Staci, she asked, "What are you wearing, punkin?"

Staci looked down at the nightshirt as though she had no idea of how it had ended up on her body. It had a screen-printed picture of a manic dinosaur driving a car with a license plate that read "I 8 NY." "Molly loaned it to me. Even though she's almost a year older than I am, we're about the same size. We can wear the same clothes. She said I can borrow some of hers until I get mine back. Isn't that great?"

"That's very nice of you, Molly."

"No problem." Molly rooted around in the refrigerator and surfaced with a big bottle of soda and a carton of chip dip. She grabbed two glasses, a box of cookies, and a bag of chips from the cabinet and swooped out of the kitchen, the force of her breathless momentum pulling Staci along in its wake.

At the door she turned. "We're going to bed now, guys. See you in the morning." She added for April's benefit, "Don't worry about hygiene and stuff. I gave Staci a toothbrush and comb. Unused, of course."

April sat there for a full moment before the impact of

the girl's words struck her. They were going to bed? She turned to Jake uncertainly. "I'm afraid the girls are presuming too much. You've been very kind to us, Mr. . . . Jake, but we can't intrude on your hospitality like this."

"Like what?" he asked innocently, thinking he owed Molly one for being such a take-charge kind of kid.

"Like staying here. There was never any discussion of arrangements, but I assumed we'd go to a motel."

Jake couldn't think of anything he wanted less right then. "A motel? I won't hear of it. Besides, how would you pay for it? I understood you lost all your money, traveler's checks, and credit cards in the robbery."

"You understood correctly." April had hoped that the man would offer her a loan until Tuesday, but his generosity toward strangers was obviously limited to a pizza dinner. And just as obvious, she certainly couldn't broach the subject of a loan herself.

"I assumed you and Staci would stay here until you got your problems solved. I hope I haven't offended you by taking too much for granted."

She was about to say that such an arrangement didn't seem quite proper when she realized that accepting money from a strange man wasn't exactly the height of propriety either. There was only one alternative, and that was to phone the Conways. She sneaked a dubious glance at her savior. When put in perspective, staying with Jake the Rake didn't seem so bad.

"I hate to impose, but clearly I don't have a lot of choices," she said with a wan smile.

He heard the bitten-back pride in her words and silently cursed himself for not offering to give her his American Express Card and a ride to the nearest motel. But he wouldn't do it because if he did, he'd have no excuse to share breakfast with her tomorrow morning. On the other hand, if it were his bacon and eggs she was eating, he'd have the most natural excuse in the world.

One of these days he'd have to atone for his selfishness,

but right now he secretly exulted in the character flaw that would keep her near.

"Please, Mrs. Conway." He paused to see if she would invite him to use her first name. She didn't. "You aren't imposing at all. Extending our home to you and Staci is the least Molly and I can do to help make up for what the Thug Welcome Wagon did. Please accept our hospitality."

She studied him. He seemed just sincere enough, just formal enough, to convince her that she had been a fool to imagine he was interested in her as a woman. By choosing the words "you and Staci" and "Molly and I," he'd told her that he thought of her only as his daughter's friend's mother. That was good.

But why did she feel so disappointed? He wasn't even the type of man who would appeal to her—if she were looking for a man. Which she wasn't. She'd mourned Caleb for two empty years, but she'd finally relinquished that part of her life to the past, where it belonged. She'd come to Florida so she and Staci could have a new life. So she could try her wings. How would she ever know what she was made of until she escaped the expectations of others? The last thing she needed was a pushy man who seemed to like being in charge.

She'd married Caleb three weeks after high-school graduation and had gone directly from the security of her parents' home to the security of her husband's. Caleb had been eight years her senior and knew exactly what he wanted from life. He had wanted April. His unconditional love had made her content to live in the little house on his parents' property, under his mother's constant surveillance.

Mrs. Conway had taken up, as her solemn duty, the task of transforming young April into the perfect farm wife, a wife who would be suitable for her only son. Caleb was happy just knowing that the dairy farm, which he worked with his father, would one day be his. Though she had sometimes chafed at their lack of freedom and privacy, April had been happy for him.

Staci arrived late in the first year of their marriage, and the baby tied April even more tightly to Mrs. Conway's apron strings. The older woman undertook the added task of teaching April how to be the perfect mother for her only grandchild. Young and uncertain, April was torn between loyalty to her husband and the desire to express her own opinions, to run her house and raise her child as she saw fit.

But because the seed of rebellion was sown so shallow, she soon adjusted to the Conway harness. April became the ideal farmer's wife, the ideal mother. As long as she hadn't asserted herself, her life had run smoothly, and she had come to rely upon that harmony. Caleb and Staci were the center of her universe, her life on the dairy a cocoon of sameness and predictability. Sometimes April had wondered if she was the only relic left in America of the pre-women's lib era, but she had never made waves.

The Conways, including Caleb, had fought the idea of her taking a "job." But when she explained to her husband that the work she had been asked to do for the school lunch program was strictly voluntary, more of a community service, and when she told him how important it was to her, Caleb had finally relented.

Hazel Conway had disparaged women who didn't get fulfillment from their families. But she'd deferred to her son's judgment, and April had had her first taste of independence. The next taste had been a long time in coming.

"April?" Jake had expected her to take her time making a decision, but she'd been silent for several moments now. He had to wonder if she were seriously contemplating going back to the police station. Surely his company was preferable to that of prostitutes, punks, and winos.

April realized with a start that she'd slipped into a pool of memories. But by dipping into the past, she was reminded that she was well above the age of consent and free, at last, to make her own decisions. She could stay in the same house with a man without indulging in what Hazel would call "hanky-panky."

She could and she would. "I'm sorry. Of course we'll be happy to accept your invitation. It's late and I'm very tired. We started driving early this morning, and with the robbery and all . . ."

"I understand completely." Jake rose and pulled out her chair. "Let's go upstairs and I'll show you the guest room. It has a connecting bath, so you'll have privacy. Staci is in Molly's room across the hall, if you want to look in on her."

She followed him through the house and upstairs, knocking lightly on Molly's closed door. When there was no answer, she peeked in and smiled at the sight of the two very young, very tired girls sound asleep in white brass-trimmed beds. Even the precocious Molly looked like the child she was with her ragged teddy bear clutched in her arms.

"I think we've heard the last of them for the night," she whispered to Jake.

He closed the door and opened the one across the hall. "Here's your room. There're plenty of towels and toiletries in the bathroom. I hope you'll be comfortable."

"I'm sure I will be." April looked down at her travel-stained jeans and wrinkled shirt. "Would you mind terribly if I washed our clothes?" she asked. "It would be nice to have something fresh to wear tomorrow."

"Of course. The utility room is at the other end of the hall."

Embarrassed that she had to discuss taking her clothes off, April said, "I hate to impose, but I'll need something to wear while they wash."

"Go in and make yourself at home and I'll be right back." As he headed for his room, his first thought was to lend her a pair of his pajamas; then he remembered that he didn't own any. Too bad. The thought of her wearing something of his against her bare skin was seductive. He yanked an oversized T-shirt out of a drawer, then put it back. On second thought, the idea of her wearing something of his against her bare skin might prove *too* seductive.

He headed downstairs to the room off the kitchen. Conchata Morales, his live-in housekeeper, wouldn't mind if he lent some of her things to April. Two weeks ago, when her father was hospitalized with a heart attack, he'd given her the money to fly to Mexico City to be with him. He'd also given her an extended paid leave. She wasn't due back for another week or so. He made a mental note to thank her for her unwitting hospitality.

He opened the closet and fished among the flamboyantly colored garments that so vividly expressed his housekeeper's personality. He found a wildly embroidered peasant dress and a red-hot nightgown that had clearly come from a mail-order catalog. Jake was amused. What kind of secret life was the perky, outspoken Conchata living, anyway? He hurried back upstairs before he had time to dwell on the thought of April wearing the filmy gown.

He rapped once on her door and she opened it immediately. "I found these things. I hope they'll fit."

She took the proffered garments and looked at them with a mixture of gratitude and disbelief. How convenient that he just happened to have some sexy lingerie lying around. Obviously, her first impression had been right. Did the man "entertain," in his home, the sort of women who wore peekaboo nightgowns and then left them behind?

"Thank you." She eased the door shut in his face with a curt "good night."

Grinning, Jake leaned against the door, his arms folded over his chest. Though her words had rung with disapproval and finality, the game wasn't over, not by a long shot.

CHAPTER THREE

"EVERYBODY SHOULD HAVE one," April mumbled to the sexy reflection in the mirror as she smoothed the lust-inspiring nightgown down over her hips. "But only if that body has a husband."

She sighed and straightened her shoulders. The movement lifted her breasts, and the gown's bodice, what little there was of it, shifted and threatened to defect. Strategically placed tassels bounced merrily and something glinted and caught her eye. Further examination revealed a tiny, gold ornament in the center of each tassel, and the total tastelessness of the garment made April giggle in spite of herself.

She wondered again who belonged to this hey-look-at-me piece of licentious lingerie. Obviously, it was someone close to Keegan. Quite close indeed. But since she was merely his reluctant houseguest, his peccadillos and perversions were none of her business. She had enough frustration in her life without getting caught up in thoughts of Jake the Rake while on her way to bed.

She turned off the bedside lamp, slipped between the smooth sheets, and lay back among the soft pillows. But despite her fatigue, her eyes seemed stuck in the open position. Try as she would, she couldn't get Jake out of her mind. It had been more years than she cared to admit since she'd been preoccupied with such fierce speculation about a man. He was more than a finely honed body, more than another handsome face. He seemed like a truly nice guy, and that made the situation worse. Though he did have questionable taste in nighttime attire.

The last thing she wanted to do was to admire him, but during the course of the evening, she'd had to reevaluate her first opinion of him. Despite his reputation as a rounder, he obviously had a special and loving relationship with his daughter. Who wouldn't think highly of that?

Staci had shared most of her letters from Molly, and April had noted that Molly had never mentioned her mother. She wrote frequently of her Aunt Mags and Uncle Fred and their "entourage of ankle biters," but on the subject of mothers, she was suspiciously silent.

April didn't understand this sudden, burning need to know about the woman who had conceived Jake's child. Maybe knowing about someone he must have loved at one time would offer the insight she needed to explain to herself why she was so attracted to him. Not that it wasn't perfectly natural and acceptable to be drawn to a virile, good-looking man like Jake. Especially when she'd been given plenty of encouragement.

All evening he'd dropped numerous, yet subtle, hints that he was interested in getting to know her better. He was sincere and open, traits that contrasted with his public image. But the most endearing thing about him was his ability to make her feel special, as if everything she said were of the utmost importance to him. He seemed to have a knack for giving a woman his undivided attention. April could only speculate on how well that ability had served him in the past.

She'd never thought of herself as anyone special, but in a short time Jake had somehow made her feel unique. He had also made her totally aware of the fact that she was a vibrant woman, and that could prove dangerous. One look into his eyes and tiny fires had erupted within her. Fires that made her forget he was a heartbreak looking for a place to happen. She couldn't afford to dwell on a man like that.

It would be so easy to let her libido rule her head, so easy to succumb to the sexual magnetism that drew her. But she had an impressionable young daughter to worry about, a business to get off the ground, and a new life to launch. No doubt about it; it would be wise to move on as soon as possible.

April willed herself to relax, to sleep. But when sleep finally came, she dreamed of a steamy, romantic fantasy starring Jake and herself. So pleasant and fulfilling was the dream that it took two bloodcurdling screams to penetrate her sleep-fogged brain and spur her into action. She recognized the agonized cries of her daughter and bolted for the door across the hall. By the time she reached it, Jake was right behind her.

They had been through the nightmare trauma before, and April knew what to do. She sat on the edge of the bed and held Staci close, crooning soothing words until the child's racking sobs eased.

"Oh, Mommy, I thought something awful had happened to you," Staci moaned.

"It was a dream, sweetheart," April whispered. "I'm here and I'm fine. It was just a bad dream."

Staci leaned back and blinked at her mother as if to make sure. "Yeah," she gasped, hugging April tightly.

Molly, who had been watching the proceedings with wide eyes, patted her friend's shoulder and said, "Oh, Staci, you nearly scared me to death."

Jake struggled to keep his gaze under control, knowing he dare not risk as much as a glance at April in the shocking nightgown. If he did, he would need another cold shower, and two in the same night were way over his limit.

His thoughts had been far from innocent when he'd left

her for the night, but since he was trying to be on his best behavior, he'd restrained his bad-boy impulses. Out in the darkened hall, he'd glimpsed her in the sexy outfit, and his good intentions had deserted him like fleas from a dipped dog.

Soft and sweet and womanly, April looked incongruous in the siren's outfit she wore, and Jake had to suppress a strong urge to wrap her in a blanket. She had spirit and heart, but she was also trusting and vulnerable... and that was the problem. She was a thinking man's bombshell. When she looked at him with those wide eyes of hers, he felt like an unprincipled libertine. Damned if she didn't bring out protective instincts he hadn't known he possessed.

He forced himself back to more immediate matters. "She seems all right now." He leaned down, retrieved an empty cookie box from the floor, wadded it into a ball, and took aim at the wastebasket across the room. He missed.

"Good shot, Pops," Molly said as he sat down on her bed.

He spied an open container of onion dip on the bedside table, a bag of potato chips spilling from under the bed, and half-consumed glasses of soft drinks. "Any one of these items could have inspired that dream." His gesture took in the leftovers. "Or it could have been the result of a wild combination thereof."

"How much of this junk did you eat before bed?" April knew the food wasn't responsible for Staci's nightmare, but she wanted to give her daughter an excuse that wouldn't have to be explained.

"I think I'm feeling better already." Staci collapsed against her pillows and smiled at her mother gratefully.

April and Jake tucked in their respective children. They both started to leave, and by the light in the hallway, she knew the exact moment that his gaze fastened to her chest.

Clearing his throat, unable to look away from the cleavage revealed by Conchata's bawdy gown, he groped for something to say and came up with, "Shall I get you some antacid to give her?"

Warmth spread through April and her breath caught. The red scrap of nylon was revealing enough. But the look in Jake's eyes when they rose slowly to meet hers made her feel as if her scantily clad body were on display. She couldn't concentrate on his question, she could only stare at him, lost. In the dim light his face was a study of perfect planes and angles, and his lips parted with just the right touch of sensual appeal.

She forced herself to answer and her voice sounded strange. "What did you say?"

"Antacid." Jake swallowed hard. Was she feeling what he felt? The heat, the need, the longing to touch? "Do you want any?" he whispered.

"Do I want any?" she repeated in an attempt to decide what he was offering. Without her permission, her gaze roamed across the wide expanse of his smooth, bare chest, which was a bas-relief of firm muscle. Then it traveled downward to his narrow hips. All he wore was a pair of athletic shorts, and the light picked out the golden hairs on his forearms and legs and made them gleam. When she saw a muscle twitch in one powerful thigh, April had a sudden urge to grab Staci and run for her life.

When she realized he was still awaiting her answer, she murmured, "No, no, thank you," in an unconvincing attempt to turn down more than the antacid.

"Are you sure?" he challenged, fully aware of how her gaze had wandered.

Something in his tone snagged her attention, and she blinked up at his face, suddenly distracted by his chin. Softly squared and proud, it bore the slightest hint of a cleft that matched the little dent near his upper lip. It became more prominent when he smiled, as he was doing now. April was confused and dismayed by the intensity of her reaction to him, but she was sure of one thing: Antacid would be no cure for the type of heartburn she would suffer at this man's hands.

A slow, crooked grin tilted his mouth, and his hungry eyes assumed a bedroom look as they prowled over her in the same slow, painstaking way she'd just studied him. She trembled, and for one reckless moment he was tempted to forget where they were and why they were there, to forget his vow to never expose Molly to any nighttime encounters. His only thought was to take April into his arms and satisfy some of the gut-twisting need wound up within him.

But then Molly spoke, and reason was restored in the nick of time. "I think the crisis is over in here." She cleared her throat. "You guys might as well go back to bed."

April blushed and blew Staci a kiss. "Are you sure you don't want me to stay a while?"

"I'm sure." She burrowed into the covers. "I'm okay."

"Want to spend the rest of the night in my room?" April suggested, a bit too hopefully.

Jake thought she was talking to him and realized he was so captivated by her that he was starting to hallucinate. He said good night and quickly left the room.

"Night, Pops," Molly called, her gaze on April.

April stalled by tucking already-snug covers securely around both girls. She kissed Staci again and without hesitation, leaned over to brush Molly's cheek with her own. "Good night, Molly."

Molly wrapped her arms around April's neck, hugging her, holding her close for just a fraction of a moment. "You smell so good, just like a mother." When the child grinned up at her, she was wearing her father's little dimple and April couldn't resist lightly kissing it.

"Thank you." April backed to the doorway and leaned against the frame for a moment, wondering if Jake had returned to his room. When she stepped into the hall and closed the door, she found out.

"Pssst," he called from the end of the hall. "Let's go downstairs and talk."

She turned her back to him and whispered over her shoulder, "I can't. I'm not dressed for talking."

"So I noticed. That's why I brought this." He tossed her a long-sleeved white shirt and told her to hurry up and put it on. "Those tassels are damn distracting and there's something I want to discuss with you."

Deeply embarrassed, April pulled on the shirt, which fell to her knees, and rolled up the sleeves. "I'm sorry Staci woke everyone," she said to remind him that it wasn't her fault she hadn't had time to cover herself properly.

"No problem. At first I thought we were under siege."

They went into a den decorated with masculine furniture and numerous athletic plaques, trophies, and awards. April sat uneasily on the deeply cushioned sofa while Jake opened a small liquor cabinet and poured two snifters of brandy.

"I don't know about you, but I need this. When I heard Staci, I imagined all sorts of gruesome things." He shook his head. "Suffice to say, my imagination conjured up some pretty hairy visions."

"I know what you mean. Nothing strikes terror into a parent's heart faster than a child's scream in the middle of the night."

"Does it happen very often?"

April sniffed the amber liquid, then sipped it appreciatively. "After her father died, the nightmares were fairly regular, but as time passed, their severity lessened and the dreams slowly tapered off. She hardly ever has them anymore."

"She seemed terrified that something had happened to you. The dream wasn't about her father's death."

"It's complicated." April stretched her neck and rolled her head to the side in an effort to relieve some of the tension. "She misses her father but also fears losing me.

Maybe the robbery triggered it, or maybe she needed reassurance that I won't abandon her, too."

"Do you think she'll ever *really* be over it?"

"I don't know, but I hope so. After Caleb's death, Staci refused to talk about him at all. If anyone so much as mentioned his name, she fled to her room. I was glad to find out that she wrote to Molly about it. She isolated herself too much."

"Did it last long?"

"Unfortunately, yes. Caleb's parents practically erected a shrine to him in their living room."

"And you two had to live there, with a monumental daily reminder of what you'd lost?"

"It wasn't their fault. Caleb was their only son and they had invested a lifetime of love in him. They just wanted to keep his memory alive. But I began to worry that Staci would never accept his death. I was frightened and discussed seeking professional help for her, but Mother Conway objected. She claimed children were tough creatures who had been getting along without psychiatrists throughout the ages."

"Yes, but now they don't have to."

"She insisted that Staci would get over it in time. I was still grieving and wanted to believe her, so I did nothing. But when the nightmares didn't go away, I realized her grief was as strong as ours and that she needed help in order to cope."

"How did you handle it?"

"I asserted myself for the first time by taking Staci to a child psychologist."

"You've been asserting yourself ever since. Right?" Jake asked gently, wondering if April felt abandoned and if she still missed her husband. "How long does it usually take for a person to recover from the death of a loved one?"

April frowned.

"I'm sorry, that was an insensitive question. I didn't mean to pry." He leaned back against the cushions and stared at the ceiling. "You don't have to answer if you don't want to. I'll understand."

"It's difficult to explain. It happened in stages for us. Once we worked through the grief, the anger, the guilt, the loneliness and all the rest, we were halfway there. When we were able to move Caleb from here," April pointed to her head, "to here," she laid her hand over her heart, "we could get on with life."

It was good to know she was ready to move ahead. Jake knew from Staci's letters to Molly that April's husband had drowned while trying to save children from a submerged school bus that had run off a rain-flooded bridge. He wasn't sure he really wanted to know, but he felt compelled to ask, "What was Caleb like?"

April looked at him to see if his question was an idle one. She saw from the look on his face that he really wanted to know. "He was a wonderful father; he and Staci were very close. Just as you and Molly are." She shrugged. "He was a devoted son and a good husband. He loved me and protected me from the world."

A wonderful father, a devoted son, but only a "good" husband. Jake thought he detected a note of sadness in April's voice, as though she might have resented being sheltered or placed third on her husband's list of priorities. "A hero," he said softly.

"Yes. He was a hero. Caleb had given up most of his independence and privacy to farm with his parents." Without realizing that she did so, April spoke her thoughts aloud. "He was always ready to give up something for others. Ultimately, what he gave up was his life."

"He must have been quite a man."

"You know," she said thoughtfully, "sometimes I wished he were a little more selfish."

Jake wondered about that. "I don't know if that's an admirable trait. It isn't the stuff heroes are made of. Take me, for example. Mags says I'm much too selfish. Even though it hasn't always seemed to be in Molly's best interest, I've kept her with me whenever possible."

"I'd call that being a caring parent." She found it difficult to believe a woman had once had Jake Keegan and given him up. And even more astounding was the fact that he hadn't been snatched up by someone else by now. Without thinking, her question just rolled out: "Where in the world is your wife?"

"I don't have one."

"Well, of course you don't now, but you must have had one at some time. Molly's mother?"

"Nope. I've never been married. I'm what the statistics call an unwed father. Molly's mother didn't want her, but I did. I'm proud of her and very, very lucky to have her as part of my life."

Jake saw the expression on April's face change. It softened and became tender, admiring, and he knew instinctively that the simple fact of responsible fatherhood had elevated him a few notches in her opinion. That was good, so why did he feel so bad? His original purpose in bringing April in here was to be open and honest about his intentions for the two of them, but he was no longer sure of what those intentions were. He couldn't seem to shake the feeling that something fateful had happened today. Was she actually that special someone he and Chaz had talked about? If so, was he ready for her?

"Molly is delightful." April hoped he would volunteer the information she was seeking. "It must have been hard to raise her all alone."

Talking about the past wasn't one of his favorite things to do, but if it would enable her to get to know him better he was all for it. "I've had a lot of help from my sister. And my friends."

That would be Aunt Mags, April decided. "What about Molly's mother?" she asked bluntly.

"It was a long time ago. I was just a kid in college and thought I was in love. When she found out she was pregnant, Shelley wanted money for an abortion, and that was before anyone agreed that fathers of unborn children had rights. I finally talked her into giving me the baby and keeping the money for herself. I had to go into major hock, but it was worth it."

April didn't attempt to hide her disapproval of Molly's mother. "I can't believe a woman could be so callous. You mean she actually sold her baby?"

"Several times now. She threatened to sue to gain custody when I signed with the Jags, but was willing to negotiate. Over the years she'd crawl out of the woodwork whenever she heard that I'd attained some new success. The last time was just a month ago, after we won the championship. Finally, my lawyer advised me not to pay, even though she threatened the nastiest custody battle of all."

"Could she have won?"

"My attorney says no, but I couldn't take even the slightest chance. Besides, something like that would hurt Molly. Right now she's happy and I don't want to foul that up over a few thousand bucks. I have plenty of money and I can always get more, but I don't know what I'd do without . . ." He stopped abruptly, his words clogged with emotion.

April reached over and patted his hand. "You did the right thing."

"The lawyer made Shelley sign a new iron-clad agreement as well as receipts for all the money I've paid her over the years. He says she won't be back, that no self-respecting attorney would take her case once he gets a look at the evidence.

"The funny thing is, in all the years that Shelley wanted something, she never said she wanted Molly. She hasn't seen her since she was a toddler, and Molly doesn't even remember what her mother looks like. I've tried to talk to Molly about it, but I don't know if she really understands."

"Does Molly know about the custody threats?"

"She's pretty perceptive, but I don't think so."

"Doesn't she ask about her mother?"

"She used to." He chuckled, remembering. "When she was small, she went through a stage of calling every woman she met 'Mama,' and that certainly made for a few embarrassing moments."

"I can imagine."

"When she became more persistent with her questions, I tried to explain that some women couldn't help it. They weren't meant to be mothers, that sometimes they just went away and it hurt too much for them to try to come back."

April shook her head. "And Molly let it go at that?"

"No, not Molly. She thought it over, then decided that what had happened to her had happened to Poor Perci."

"Who's Perci?"

"Poor Perci," he corrected. "He's a pup our friends rescued from their neighbor's poodle. After giving birth, his mother, Babette, took one sniff of her lone offspring and refused to clean him or to let him nurse. Poor Perci would have died if Chaz and Ivy hadn't hand-raised him."

"Now I see why he's called Poor Perci." She recalled Molly's hug and her remark about April smelling like a mother. She shared it with Jake.

"It's all a manifestation of her need for a mother figure. I've tried to be honest with her, but I wanted her to know that Shelley's behavior wasn't really a rejection of her. Since she was only four at the time, Poor Perci's plight was something she could understand."

"What does she think now?"

"She hasn't brought it up in years." He ran his hands through his hair and stood abruptly. Pacing the floor, he continued, "But there's a complication. When Poor Perci grew out of the puppy stage, Babette became more tolerant and allowed him to bask in her exalted company from time to time. Molly latched on to the idea that when she grew up, her own mother would do the same. I'm afraid she might be waiting for Shelley to accept the grown-up Molly and that's the reason she acts the way she does. Being a child hasn't been much fun for her."

"That sounds completely unbearable." April wiped a stray tear from her cheek and pretended to massage her temples so Jake wouldn't notice. But he did.

"All this serious discussion given you a headache? I can fix that." He strode across the room, stood behind the couch, and began to massage the back of her head and neck with his thumbs. "I have magic hands," he said, grateful for the diversion and for the chance to touch her. "Everyone says so."

"I'll just bet they do." April melted into the sofa as his large hands slipped inside the neck of the shirt and his thumbs and fingers kneaded her nape. "How do you manage to juggle so many women without mishap?"

"Don't believe everything you hear. I've never been much for zone defense. I prefer one on one," he said suggestively.

"Do tell," she scoffed.

"It's true."

"That's not why they call you Jake the Rake."

"Ahh," he sighed. "Those were the days! I suppose that in my youth I might have trod on a few hearts."

"Might have?" she teased.

"Okay, I'll admit I stepped out a bit when all the fame first struck. I began dating with a vengeance. You know, heavy, world-class stuff. Weekend jaunts to Paris or a night of dancing in New York. Romantic stuff. All that effort wasted on women whose attention span didn't last as long as the five-second buzzer."

She gave him a sidelong look. "How ungrateful of them."

Jake grinned sheepishly. "I tired of it soon enough, but too late. The damage was done. I had a reputation to uphold."

April pursed her lips and nodded. "So you've retired the dancing shoes for good?"

"That's right," he replied self-righteously.

"Why then do I get the feeling that your hormones just kept right on waltzing?"

"On the contrary. They've become very selective about their dance partners now." Jake didn't tell her what he really felt. None of those women had ever tugged at his heartstrings, made him buckle at the knees, made his throat tighten or his head spin. She would think him certifiable if he admitted on such short acquaintance that she did all those things to him. He kept his mouth shut and worked his fingers over her taut muscles.

April's skin grew heated under his touch and became a conduit for shivery sensations that ran down her back. She was supposed to relax, but her stomach tightened. She wondered what it would be like to have those large, capable hands on her entire body. She shook her head to free it of such forbidden thoughts. Helpless, she did nothing to stop him when his firm, tension-easing massage slipped into what could more accurately be called a caress.

She closed her eyes and prayed he'd stop, but Jake kept right on soothing her neck and shoulders until she was little more than a shuddering tangle of sensation. Much more of this and April feared she would abruptly pull him down beside her to have her way with him. There was definitely magic in his hands, she decided as her head lolled back. She looked up into his passion-darkened eyes and knew that it was too late.

Jake stared down at her and lazily stroked her throat. He recognized, in this auburn-haired female, all the qualities he admired. She was funny, smart, and good. And she was beautiful. Her soft pink lips parted, and he ached with longing.

"Where . . ." April paused, concentrating harder as his face drew nearer, "did you learn . . ."—he was going to kiss her; she could see it in his eyes— "to do that?"

She should protest, tell him to stop, beg him to stop, but she did nothing more than moisten her lips as his slowly descended toward hers. She didn't really want him to stop. One kiss couldn't hurt. She'd think of it as a special moment. After all she'd been through today, she deserved it. His mouth moved closer, and closer.

She was overwhelmed by sweet anticipation, and her breath seemed to stop when their lips finally met. His mouth was warm and exciting, his tongue gentle but insistent as it sought admittance. He tasted just as she thought he would, of brandy with a hint of toothpaste. It felt wonderful, and right. April relaxed against the sofa, and with her hand on the back of his neck, pulled him closer so she could return the kiss.

It was as good as he'd thought it would be. Stuck behind the couch, Jake cursed himself as a fool for having put himself in such a position. He wanted, needed, to deepen the kiss, to wrap her in his arms, to pull her body next to his. He wanted to taste her bare skin, to make love to her. And he sensed that she wanted it, too. But that wasn't possible, not while he was standing behind the sofa.

He took a chance and did the only thing he knew to do. By levering himself with his arms, he swung his legs over to kneel beside her on the sofa without breaking lip contact.

April's eyelids fluttered open when she felt the sudden shift, his nose crossing hers. Their mouths smiled against one another and Jake growled softly, the sound rumbling from deep within his chest.

Free to follow through now, he stretched out over her, careful not to let his weight hurt her. His hand was gentle as he stroked her full breast through two layers of fabric. Instinctively, he moved to unbutton her shirt.

April had been so caught up in the magic of Jake's kiss that she'd let things go too far. When she realized what was happening, she twisted away, and pushing on his chest, tried to wriggle out from under him.

"Sorry, Jake, but it won't work."

"Sure it will," he cajoled. "We just got off to a bad start

because I was a little overanxious. Let me try again. I promise it'll be better from this angle."

"I don't doubt it for a moment," she agreed.

She was shocked by her reaction: a nearly overwhelming urge to give herself up to him, to surrender to his masterful touch. He was right, it would be better this way, their bodies free to melt against each other, his thigh free to wedge between hers. But she couldn't submit to this man. She hardly knew him. Caleb was the only man she'd ever made love to, and logically she knew that what was happening was wrong. The sensual side of her life was sadly lacking, but she couldn't afford to fill the void with Jake.

Straightening up, she leaned back against the sofa, took a deep breath, and turned to face him. "I'm sorry," she said, "but I'm just not ready. I'm not sure I ever will be."

"Don't worry, April. I understand," he reassured her, settling himself beside her. But he didn't understand. How could she pull back when it felt so right? He berated himself for rushing her. He had a lot to learn when it came to courting; he had never had to do much of it.

"I may be stranded here, but that doesn't mean I ... I ..."

"I wouldn't dream of doing anything you don't want me to do. It was only a kiss. Nothing to get excited about."

"True, but I wish it hadn't happened," she lied. To Jake it might be no more than a brief encounter, but it had been much more than that to her. "Maybe I should leave in the morning." If she had to call the Conways so she could escape his magnetism, so be it.

Jake sighed. "I'm harmless, Red. I haven't been reduced to forcing my unwanted attentions on women yet." He smiled what he hoped was a harmless smile and shrugged.

"You said you wanted to talk to me," she reminded him briskly, as if he hadn't just kissed her senseless.

"Oh, yes," Jake stalled. It would be a tactical error to

express his interest too soon. First he had to show her what a great guy he could be. Inspiration struck. "I was thinking. Well... it's pretty obvious to me that we need each other."

"Is that right?" she asked skeptically.

"The restaurant," he explained. "Since we both have ambitions to be restaurateurs, maybe we should form a partnership. The timing is perfect and it's a great match. You need a gimmick and a backer, and I can provide both." He spoke as if it were settled. "We need each other."

"You're busy being a jock. Remember?"

"I'm getting old. I want out before all those kids kill me. What better time to retire than when I'm still a champ? What do you say?"

"I don't know much about sports."

"Not about that, about the restaurant."

"No." April stood and paced the length of the room. "Don't you see, it would happen all over again. I'd be letting another person take over. As a child, I tried to please my father, as a wife—my husband. When Caleb was gone, my mother-in-law wanted me to do things her way."

"I'm not—"

April stopped him. "If you backed the restaurant and used your celebrity status to influence its success, the whole thing would be yours. I may not succeed on my own, but I need to try. I have to do this myself. It's my turn. It's time for me to take control of my own life."

"Okay, okay. No hard feelings. I understand. Perfectly. It was just a suggestion." He grinned hopefully and was rewarded with a tremulous smile.

He stood up and holding out his hand, asked, "Can we still be friends?"

April took it, knowing that her reaction had been the result of years of repressed feelings. It was also a latent response to the passions Jake had released within her. "It was very sweet of you to offer all that to a stranger, and I don't want you to think that I'm ungrateful, Jake. I'm sorry if I came on too strong."

"That's okay, April. You have every right to be overwrought. You've been through a lot today." Their gazes caught and held.

"You've been a great help, and I do appreciate it," she went on. "But I owe myself this chance, and I just wanted you to understand that." What she wanted was for him to kiss her again.

"I do, Red." Jake couldn't decode her mixed signals. He could have sworn that she was waiting for him to make a move, but she had told him she wasn't ready and he didn't want to screw this up—it was much too important. Not knowing what else to do, he squeezed her hand reassuringly.

"Thanks for everything, Jake," she stalled. She shouldn't have told him she wasn't ready. April had a feeling that he was just persistent enough to wait for her to retract that statement, no matter how long it might take.

"Any time," he answered.

She tried to remove her hand from his grasp, but he brought it to his lips and kissed her knuckles—one at a time, with agonizing thoroughness—before setting her free and favoring her with one of his heart-stopping grins.

April backed slowly to the stairway. "So, good night."

Jake nodded. "Good night, April."

She fled up the stairs and turned at her door to find him right behind her. "Thanks for everything," she repeated unnecessarily.

"You bet." Jake winked. "Any time you need me, just whistle."

April closed the door in his face and heard his answering chuckle. His bedroom door opened, then closed. As she crawled into bed, she realized that she was still wearing his shirt. It smelled of him and gave her a special feeling. She got up and took off the silly nightgown, then slipped his shirt back on.

She liked the crisp starchiness of it against her bare skin.

CHAPTER FOUR

THE NEXT MORNING, April followed the aroma of freshly brewed coffee into the kitchen and found Jake and the girls busy preparing breakfast. Bright Florida sunshine streamed through the bay window in the breakfast nook, where Staci was arranging blue-plaid place mats on the table, and washed over Jake and Molly, who stood at the counter. He was manning the electric waffle iron and she was pouring milk and juice.

April stood unobserved in the doorway as Jake regaled the giggling girls with terrible "knock-knock" jokes, and their delighted laughter warmed her heart. Judging from their damp swimsuits, they'd all had an early dip in the pool that lay glistened just outside the French doors. Although April tried not to notice how good Jake looked in his red Speedo, the brevity of it made that task practically impossible. Fortunately, the striped shirt he wore concealed the muscles she knew rippled beneath when he stretched to fish a fork out of a drawer.

The three were so caught up in their fun that they didn't notice her, and April watched for several moments before announcing her presence. She'd planned to work out other living arrangements today, but their easy camaraderie reminded her that there was more at stake here than just her own feelings.

"Good morning, everyone," she said at last.

"Good morning, sleepyhead," Jake replied. His good-natured grin was infectious, and April smiled back.

"It's a good thing you got up when you did, Mom. Jake's been telling us about his sure-fire method for getting lazybones out of bed in a hurry."

April raised one brow. "Is that right?"

"It's the old ice-water dousing trick," Molly explained. "Take it from a former victim, it's shocking but painless." She sat down beside Staci and poured maple syrup on her waffle.

Seeing her for the first time in broad daylight, Jake was struck again by April's loveliness, by how *fresh* she looked. She wore no makeup and her squeaky-clean hair was left to curl as it would. She was definitely a daytime lady. Sunshine suited her.

"Frankly, I was looking forward to it." Jake's wink drew a surprised look from April. "First I planned to rip off your covers—all the better to wet you down, my dear." He was being the Big Bad Wolf. "Then..." He paused long enough to throw in a devilish leer. "Perhaps I shouldn't reveal all my secrets; it might spoil the fun next time."

"Assuming there will be a next time," April put in dryly.

"There will be," he told her with the same confidence he'd displayed about everything else. "Actually, I'd hate to resort to such tactics, but if it ever comes down to a choice between a wet mother and cold waffles, you won't stand a chance." He pulled out her chair before sitting down.

"If it was a reaction you wanted, you would have been disappointed," April scoffed.

Jake glanced at the girls to make sure they were otherwise occupied, then turned the full heat of his gaze on her. "On the contrary, I think I would have been delighted."

April ignored his remark. "I'll have you know I wasn't

lolling in bed. I was busy trying to clean the convenience-store crud from our clothes." She gestured at the short peasant dress she wore and added, "It'll be nice to get back into my own clothes. At least they fit."

Molly swallowed the food in her mouth and took a swig of her milk. Then, pointing an accusing finger at her father, she scolded, "You borrowed some of Conchata's clothes, didn't you, Pops?"

Jake stared at his daughter through the tines of his fork and intoned, "Brilliant deduction, Dr. Watson. What gave me away, old boy? Last night's kinky nightgown, or this morning's daring mini?"

"Both, my good man," Molly intoned right back. "Just wait till she hears you let someone wear her clothes, no offense, April. Conchata's gonna kill you."

Molly's revelation wasn't particularly comforting, but at least April now knew who belonged to the clothes. She didn't know who Conchata might be or what she meant to Molly and Jake, but she must be someone special if Molly recognized her clothing. A nameless, faceless female had been bad enough, but April felt inexplicably disappointed now that Jake's "friend" had a name and a personality.

"Mayhem?" Jake clucked. "Maybe. But she'll get over it. Besides, none of us would be so indelicate as to tell her, now would we?"

The girls looked at each other and burst into laughter.

He leveled his playful glare at Staci. "Would we?"

Staci sat up straight and made a zipping motion across her lips. Jake turned to Molly, who was still convulsed by a fit of giggles. "Would we?" he insisted.

"She won't hear it from me." Molly held up her hand as if swearing allegiance.

"Maybe it would help if I explained," April offered.

Jake and Molly glanced at each other with look-alike grins. "Bad idea," they answered as one.

April didn't understand the leaden feeling in her stomach when she thought of Jake and the hot-tempered Conchata together; she tried to tell herself it was because her first impression had been correct after all. He was what Hazel Conway would have called a libertine, and she had been a fool to think those kisses last night had meant a thing to him.

"I'm sure if I explained what happened, she would understand. Will she be coming over here today?"

"She's in Mexico or else she'd be here now." Molly's tone was matter-of-fact. "She lives here."

"I see." April's voice sounded hollow to her own ears and she ducked her head to concentrate on her waffle. He was living with another woman, and in her absence, had not only invited April into his home, but into his arms as well. He was worse than a libertine. Just when she had decided to reevaluate her opinion of him, he had turned out to be the indifferent womanizer she'd suspected he was all along. April glanced at him, wondering if she would ever figure him out.

"When do you expect her back?" she asked.

"It's hard to tell with Conchata." Jake knew that April had leaped to all the wrong conclusions; her expressions gave away her every thought. He started to correct her but then reconsidered. A little friendly competition might be just the ticket. If she was as disinterested in him as she claimed to be, she wouldn't mind another woman.

He assumed an expression of boyish innocence and decided to let her think the worst for just a little longer. "She's a free spirit, if you know what I mean."

"I see." April cut into her waffle with a vengeance. How convenient that Jake had failed to mention his housemate before this. The woman didn't have much taste in clothes, but April had to feel sorry for her. Clearly, Jake was the out-of-sight, out-of-mind type. In an effort to conceal her feelings, she kept quiet and tried to figure out how she could remove Staci and herself from Jake Keegan's lecherous clutches.

It only took a moment for Jake to realize that his failure

to tell the whole truth had backfired. Since April's reaction was even stronger than he'd hoped, he wasted no time in setting her straight. "Conchata's a bit flighty at times, but she's a heckuva housekeeper. She's been with us for five years."

The news caught April in mid-swallow and she nearly choked. Recovering, she asked, "Conchata's a live-in housekeeper?"

Jake smiled. "Of course. What did you think she was?"

Since that question couldn't be answered in front of impressionable children, April shrugged to show how little she cared one way or another. It bothered her that she'd let it affect her in the first place, and she silently chastised herself for practically broadcasting her feelings to Jake.

Jake didn't miss the look of relief on April's face when she learned who Conchata was. It had been a long time since anything had gratified him so much. Offering her another waffle, he urged, "Eat up, Red. You'll need your strength. I've got big plans for us today."

"What kind of plans?" It didn't matter. Now that April knew Conchata wasn't Jake's live-in paramour, she could afford to be magnanimous.

"I thought I'd take you girls to the mall. Molly always says that when the going gets tough, the tough go shopping. We'll pick up a few items for you and Staci. What do you say?"

"You've already done enough for us, Jake." Although she couldn't think of anything she'd enjoy more than spending the day with this irresistible father-and-daughter team, April felt honor-bound to resist. "I can't let you buy us things."

"If it will make you feel better, you can pay me back on Tuesday. The Jags' owner, Harry Tanner, invited us to celebrate the Fourth at his barbecue, and you'll need some clothes to tide you over until the banks open, won't you?"

April didn't have a chance to argue about attending a party with Jake, even though she could think of several good objections without even trying. When she attempted to voice them, Jake and the girls double-teamed her. In the final analysis, she lost without putting up a fight.

Never having shopped with a man before, April found the outing entertaining as well as educational. Caleb had always begged off completely, or waited impatiently in the car. On the rare occasions when he did need to buy something for himself, her husband had gone directly to the store that he knew sold the item, purchased it quickly, and left in the same manner. Window-shopping, according to Caleb, was a big waste of time.

Jake was another story. He actually seemed to enjoy himself, and steered her and Staci through the busy department store with ease. He made sure they avoided the budget departments, and he and Molly became their on-the-spot fashion consultants. If he wasn't having fun, April decided, he was darned proficient at faking a good time.

The girls, however, did not share his long-term enthusiasm. Once their shopping was done, they became bored and restless. Molly sighed dramatically. "How much longer? I want to go to the record store."

Jake and April exchanged exasperated parental glances; then Jake firmly guided them to a quiet corner. "Look, girls, we were patient while you oohed and aahed over the pre-teens. Right?"

Molly began, "Yeah, but—"

"No buts," Jake insisted, then turned to Staci. "Right, Stace?"

"I guess so," Staci said, relenting.

"Then you two will kindly stop complaining. Give April a chance to shop, and after she picks out a few things, we can stop at the record store. Then I'll take all of you to lunch at the Big Onion. Anybody have a problem with that?"

The girls brightened. "Come on, then. What are we

waiting for?" Molly pointed at a rack of miniscule juniors' swimsuits. "That's first on the list."

"I don't need a bathing suit," April demurred.

"Are you kidding?" Jake asked in an incredulous voice. "You're in Florida now. Swimwear is the official state costume. Besides, you'll need one for Harry's party."

"About that party," April began before her daughter interrupted.

"How about this one?" Staci held up a scrap of black Lycra.

April rejected it for a perfectly legitimate reason. "It's cut too low in front."

Staci grabbed another from the rack. "This one?"

April shook her head. "Cut too high on the hips."

"How about a two-piece?" Molly's look was innocence personified when she held up a yellow ruffled bikini with lime-green polka dots.

April laughed and Jake scowled. "Those suits are made for girls. What we need is one suitable for a woman." He strode to another rack and motioned for April to join him. He rifled through the swimsuits as though he knew exactly what he was looking for and finally handed her his selection. He smiled smugly. "Perfect, huh?"

She took one look at the sleek silver snakeskin-patterned suit and shook her head. "Why don't I find something a little less attention-grabbing? Like this?" She held up a plain blue maillot.

All three of them booed her choice. "That one would be great for a swim meet, April," Molly told her. "But for a party?"

"About that party. . ."

Jake draped the silver suit over her arm. "Try this one on."

"I don't know," she said skeptically. Even with its matching Chinese-silk skirt, the suit was too revealing. "This isn't something a woman from Iowa would wear."

"But you're not in Iowa now," Jake reminded her.

Recognizing a conspiracy when she saw one, April went into the dressing room fully expecting to hate the exotic swimwear. She didn't have the hard-bodied look the suit required, but when she tried it on, she realized that Jake had been right. It *was* perfect. The sensuous feel of the sleek fabric against her skin stimulated erotic flights of fancy, and she liked it.

The turtleneck and cut-in shoulders drew attention away from breasts she'd always thought too large to be chic. The leg openings were cut high on the thigh and elongated her legs, which she decided were not bad for a thirty-year-old mother. She'd have to work on her tan, but the overall effect was stunning.

She could scarcely believe the bright-eyed woman in the mirror was herself. She turned this way and that to check all angles and was amazed at her new appearance. She'd never been fashion-conscious; back home there had been no time to worry about style. But being with Jake made her aware of herself, of her body. It wasn't a bad feeling.

She came out of the dressing room a few moments later and handed the swimsuit to the salesclerk. "I'll take it."

"What changed your mind?" Jake asked.

Since she could hardly tell him the part about erotic fantasies, she merely said, "It's a good fit."

Jake gave the clerk his charge card, then turned to April with a satisfied look on his face. "I have good taste, huh?"

"You have expensive taste," she corrected.

"I can afford it," he said without hesitation, giving April the impression that he was talking about more than the purchase just made.

Jake steered her to the accessories department and insisted she have a stack of silver-and-copper-toned bracelets, bangle earrings, and metallic-colored sandals to complete the outfit. It was a good thing he was with her, because none of the purchases were what she would have made if left to her own devices.

He was helpful, complimentary, and entirely too much

fun as he helped her select a couple of casual outfits and dresses. He steered her away from the tailored styles she usually wore, and April was surprised at the effect the bright, feminine clothes had on her self-image, to say nothing of her self-confidence. Maybe clothes didn't make the man, or the woman, but the right ones could certainly make a difference.

When they came to the lingerie department, April had to put her foot down. "I think I can choose my own underwear, thank you very much," she told him. She blushed and turned her back on him when he urged her not to buy "any of that utilitarian stuff." Not that he'd ever know what she selected, but April surprised herself by scorning the practical in favor of the frivolous.

After they left the mall, they took a short tour of Jacksonville and then stopped for lunch at the Big Onion. The restaurant was owned by Joe Castelli, a former Hoosier basketball coach and long-time sports crony of Jake's. Joe made his fellow Midwesterners welcome, and April immediately liked the kindly older man who seemed to have a special place in his heart for Jake and Molly.

After a traditional cheeseburger and french-fry lunch, the girls begged quarters for the video games in the back and disappeared. April and Jake lingered over their coffee.

"This is really a nice place, Jake," April commented nervously, wishing he would move now that the girls had left the booth across from them empty. No such luck.

"I thought you'd like it. But nice? Is that all you can say about it? I was hoping you'd be positively smitten."

April smiled at the way he had of making everything sound risqué. If she lowered her guard with this man, she'd be in big trouble quicker than he could wink at a pretty girl. "The place has possibilities."

"Possibilities? With the right decor, some discreet lighting, and privacy corners, the effect would be dramatic. Joe's speciality has always been plain, great-tasting food, but with a woman's touch, this place could be a gold mine." Jake warmed to his subject. "It's in a great location, with easy access to the mall. There's lots of parking and a steady clientele."

His knowledge and enthusiasm drew a surprised look from April. "I'm not just another pretty face," he teased. "I have an MBA, and difficult as it is to be modest, I think you should know," he paused to polish his nails on his chest, "that I was on the dean's list for the four years it took me to finish grad school."

April whistled softly. "I'm impressed."

Jake nudged her with his elbow. "But don't tell anyone. My fan mail dropped twenty-three percent when one of the local sports writers called me an intellectual athlete."

"I guess I missed that one. What else did he say?"

His smile was sardonic. "She. The writer was a woman. Not much. She chose not to mention I worked part-time, went to school on a basketball scholarship, and was a single parent. In fact, she didn't dwell on my accomplishments at all. Like most writers, she preferred to describe other . . . uh . . . more sensational aspects of my life."

April knew Jake was trying to make light of it, but the look in his eye was grim. She was more confused than ever and wondered for the umpteenth time since she had met him exactly who Jake Keegan really was. "You've done a wonderful job with Molly. I really am impressed, Jake," she said sincerely.

He was tempted to encourage her compassion but smiled mockingly instead. "Finally! Something about me you like. Does this mean we can go steady?"

April pretended to think it over, all the while noting the hungry gleam in his eyes. Tension grew through the silence and she felt heat rise to her cheeks. "This is much too sudden, sir," she said with feigned coyness.

"I'm in kind of a hurry, I suppose." He traced tiny circles on the tablecloth, his fingers drawing ever nearer to her hand, resting beside her cup. "If you don't want to go steady, how about a dinner date then?"

"No," she said softly.

"Why not?" he asked equally softly as his fingers feathered over hers.

"Because you're who you are and I'm who I am."

It was impossible to think straight when Jake was sitting so close, his thigh pressed against hers in the small booth. So close that she could feel the heat from his body, smell the tantalizing scent of his expensive cologne. All of her sensory-input channels were jammed with awareness of him, and the touch of his hand on hers threatened to make her melt like ice cream on a hot boardwalk.

"Well," he drawled, "as far as rejections go, that one doesn't leave much room for argument, does it?"

"It wasn't meant to."

"What do you mean exactly?"

"I mean, I have to wonder why a man who could have any girl he wanted, and probably has, would be interested in a thirty-year-old widowed mother of one."

His hand continued its feathery massage. "Is that how you think of yourself? As a widowed mother of one?"

"It's what I am, Jake. I'm nothing like the girls you're used to."

"Maybe that's what I like about you. Has it occurred to you that I may not want a girl? That maybe I want a woman?"

His words were spoken so softly that April had to lean closer to hear them. When she did, she felt his next words as a warm breath against her cheek. His voice caressed her senses just as the finger he trailed up her arm caressed her skin, sending her pulses into a frenzy. "Have you considered, Red, that the woman I want is you?"

"Don't, Jake." She scooted away from him, totally unequipped to deal with the polished, but no doubt phoney, line he was handing her. "I may not be as sophisticated as you are, but don't insult my intelligence with such nonsense."

"What makes you think it's nonsense?"

"Because you don't know me. You know nothing about me. I'm just another challenge to you, albeit a very convenient one."

"Don't you believe in fate?"

"Only as it pertains to fortune cookies."

"Aren't you at all curious about the forces that brought us together?"

"Not really. If I never see those two young thieves again, it'll be too soon."

"Don't you find it amazing that thirty-six hours ago neither of us knew the other existed, and then wham, out of the blue we're together like this?"

April looked up in alarm. "Like what?"

"Like this." Jake's warm brown eyes looked directly into her cool blue ones as his hand cupped the back of her neck and drew her closer. April felt every frenetic beat of her heart as his gaze flickered to her lips, then back to her eyes. He leaned closer and his lips, warm and moist, touched hers. Her hands went to his chest in a token protest, but Jake urged her gently and smoothly, never demandingly, until April lost herself in the slow, melting kiss.

Jake released a deep, audible sigh against her lips. It was a coffee-flavored stream that like a whirlpool pulled her into a dark cave of sensation. She opened her lips and he accepted the invitation, stroking her mouth with mind-dissolving intimacy.

"April, April, April." The words buzzed against her lips like languid honey bees.

Her eyes fluttered open and she drew away from him. She glanced around in embarrassment, but fortunately it was past the regular lunch hour and the few people in the restaurant were reading newspapers or talking. How could she have allowed herself to be swept away like this in a moment of emotional insanity? She removed his hand from her neck self-consciously.

"This is a public place," she murmured.

Jake looked around as if he'd been beamed there without his knowledge. "So it is. We'll continue this at another time, in another place more conducive to fateful events."

"No," she said firmly. "It isn't fair for you to take advantage of me this way."

"Is that what I was doing?"

"You know it was. I don't know what to do with you."

"May I make a few suggestions?"

"I'm not ready for a relationship, and even if I were, it wouldn't be with you," she said quietly.

He looked at her thoughtfully. "Why not? Do you find me that disagreeable?"

"I don't find you disagreeable at all and you know it. But I don't have the experience to cope with a man like you. I don't even want to try." She stared at her cup. "I've had a good time today, but you overwhelm me..." Her voice trailed off. In no way could she admit the extent of his effect on her. "I don't want to get involved with you."

He watched the color run up her face and knew she was denying an attraction she felt as strongly as he did. "Don't lie, Red. You can deny it, protest it, reject it, but don't ever lie about it." Her eyes pleaded with him to let it go. Knowing that he would never get anywhere by forcing her into a showdown, he nodded in quiet acceptance. "We can take it as slow as you want. Maybe we can do this again sometime."

April took a deep breath, and Jake quickly added, "Without the kissing."

The girls returned and saved her from having to make further comment. When they rose to leave, Joe came over to say good-bye. "This restaurant is just what I've been looking for," April told the proprietor. "Would you consider selling it?"

Joe glanced briefly at Jake, then said, "I would, ma'am, but didn't Jake tell you about our agreement?" Joe ignored Jake's sharp head shake. "See, I got into trouble a few years back, took up some bad habits I couldn't kick. I nearly lost the place, but Jake put me in rehab and bailed me out of debt."

"Hell, Joe, a simple no would have been sufficient," Jake said before the man had a chance to tell it all.

"I appreciate all you done for me, Jake, and you told me the best way I could pay you back was to sell you this place when you got ready to retire. You promised it wouldn't be much longer, but I'm still waiting." He turned to April. "Jake Keegan's just about the finest human being I know. He helped me with money, time, and caring. Even ran this place during the off-season while I was taking the cure."

"Let's get out of here, before Joe gets me canonized," Jake joked self-consciously.

"I can never repay you, man," Joe replied. "I owe you."

"I'll send you a bill next week." Jake clapped Joe on the back. "Stay out of trouble, my friend."

The trip home was quiet. Jake seemed preoccupied with his thoughts, and the girls whispered and giggled in the backseat. April had plenty of time to try to piece together the puzzle that was Jake Keegan. To the media, he was Casanova; to Joe, a certified saint; and to Molly, he was father extraordinaire. The roles contradicted one another and she was more confused than ever. But in the end, it didn't really matter what she thought of him. He was not for her.

April had plans to retreat to her room and escape the smoldering looks Jake flashed her way, but as soon as they pulled into the drive, the girls badgered their parents into going swimming. After an hour of underwater tag, water basketball, and general tomfoolery, April retired to a poolside chaise. Under cover of the umbrella, she pretended to douse herself with the sunscreen Jake had thoughtfully provided. What she was really doing was watching Jake.

He was stretched out in the sun beside the diving board, coaching the girls in proper diving techniques. His sunburnished skin was sleek with oil, and the light reflecting off the pool lit up the fine golden hairs on his forearms and legs. He rested on one hip with one leg extended, the weight of his upper torso supported by an arm. His other arm rested on the leg that was bent at the knee; it was a pose April was sure she had once seen in a museum featuring statues of Greek Olympians.

Physically, he was the most perfectly beautiful man she had ever met, and she wondered again how much of her response to him was due to undiluted hormones. After all, she hardly knew him. As she watched him, her stomach tightened and she realized with startling clarity that she had never wanted anyone more. And worst of all, she wanted him not as much for what he was, but for how he made her feel when she was with him.

April had proven herself as a wife, a mother, and hopefully she would prove herself soon as a businesswoman. Yet she was still behaving like a frightened virgin when she was with Jake. She was a strong and capable woman, and she could darn well keep her hands off him for another forty-eight hours. Of course, it would help if they were tied behind her back.

As she watched, Jake laughed and pushed himself to his feet. "Keep practicing, girls. You might make the Olympics yet." Coming over and dropping into the chair next to her, he said, "I wish I had half their stamina."

April wished he had stayed where he was. "How can you say that? You're an athlete."

"I'm an old man. I'm ready to settle down." It was only as he said the words that he knew they were true. "At thirty-three, I'm pushing the limit in pro sports and I'm tired of all the traveling around. Not only that, but adolescence is a difficult time of life and I'd like to be here for Molly, to help her get through it with as little damage as possible."

April asked skeptically, "And is buying Joe's place your idea of settling down?"

"Something like that, but that's only part of it." Jake studied her. "Was your offer serious?"

"It was until I found out that you and Joe have an understanding about it. I wouldn't think of trying to buy it out from under you."

"Why not? All's fair in love and war. And business." There had always been an assumption on the part of both men that Jake would someday own the Onion. He still wanted that, but he also wanted April to have it. It would be a link between them. "I say again that the best solution is a partnership, purely platonic and strictly business."

"I'm not interested. I've traveled over a thousand miles to gain a little independence and I don't intend to give it up now. I'm sure there are other places. I've been in Jacksonville for only twenty-four hours. It may take a few days to find perfection," she said with a laugh.

Jake watched her intently. "Sometimes it only takes a few moments." He was still mystified by his feelings for this unusual woman. He hadn't even realized that he'd had standards for the women in his life until he'd met April. Nor had he ever worried about measuring up to anyone else's standards. But now, as he searched her eyes, he was afraid he might be found lacking.

"I know a little bit about what you're going to be up against. You may have trouble getting the financing you need on your own."

"I don't need financing. I have money," she defended.

"The first rule of good business is never to risk your own money on any project."

"I believe in my ability to make it. After all, if I didn't, how could I expect a backer or a banker to do so?"

"The banks probably won't touch it with a ten-foot pole because of loan restrictions. A backer might be interested in a tax shelter. If the restaurant succeeds, it's just another feather in his cap. So you put up half and you find a backer to put up the other half. If the project fails, you haven't lost everything and you both get the tax write-off."

"That's ridiculous."

"I have every faith in you as far as running a restaurant goes—the menu planning, the buying, the preparation. But reaching that point will be expensive. The kind of place you're talking about won't come cheap to begin with, and the hidden expenses will kill you. Let me give you just a sample." Jake hated to burst her bubble but she had to know what she was up against, and by the time he had finished speaking, he knew that she was feeling pretty low.

April had already considered all the pros and cons and didn't like having the cons detailed again. "Thanks for the information. I understand what you mean by not taking the risk alone. I'll talk to my bank on Tuesday, and since it's a branch of our bank back home, I'm sure I won't have any trouble."

"If you won't let me back you in the Onion, I can at least put in a good word for you with Joe. He'll listen to me."

"You'd do that? I thought that was going to be your place someday."

"Someday is the operative word here. I'm not sure of my plans right now, but you seem to be sure of yours. Think it over and go talk to Joe again."

"Maybe I'll do that. Thanks for the tip. It seems you're always doing things for me." No more was said on the subject, and a few minutes later she asked, "Would you mind if I made a couple of local telephone calls?"

"Not at all. Feel free to call the Conways as well."

"That won't be necessary."

"Hell, April, even E.T. had to call home," he teased.

"Right again," she conceded and went inside.

April telephoned the real-estate company she had rented from and asked if there was any chance that her apartment might be ready before the fifteenth. She got the answer she had expected: that there was no chance at all.

Jake and the girls came in from the pool and went to the

kitchen to begin dinner while April dialed one more number, this time to check on the belongings she had sent ahead with the moving company. In another absurd twist of fate, she was informed that all of her worldly possessions were temporarily misplaced somewhere in the warehouse, because of a computer failure. But not to worry, the man on the phone assured her, they would surely turn up sooner or later.

On that happy note, she called the Conways to let them know that she and Staci had arrived safely. Even long-distance, she could feel the disapproval of her mother-in-law and was more convinced than ever that she had done the right thing by leaving. She was careful not to mention the robbery, and motioned Staci over to talk to her grandparents.

She went back to the kitchen and leaned against the counter, massaging her temples. Jake leaned over as he took steaks out of the refrigerator and murmured in her ear, "Want me to take care of that headache for you?"

"You keep those magic fingers to yourself," April whispered furiously. "Last night was no remedy, it was a seduction."

Jake winked. "Got rid of your headache, didn't I?"

After dinner the girls disappeared into Molly's room, and as soon as the dishes were done, April excused herself for an early night. She used the pretext of reading the new paperback she had picked up at the mall, but she didn't really expect to get much reading done. Jake would see to that. She had known him for only a short time and already he had taken to haunting her thoughts as well as her dreams, both night and day.

It would be foolish to sit in that masculine den of his, surrounded by all those awards, and pretend to read about the exploits of a fictional hero when the real thing was lounging on the couch beside her. Better to put some space between them. They said their good nights and she went to her room. But she didn't get far in her book. Jake Keegan was a hard man to ignore, present or not.

Sunday passed quietly. April called the police station, and according to Sergeant Sandusky, there were still no leads on her car. He advised her to stop by that Tuesday and pick up a copy of the police report to send to her insurance company.

She also called Suze McGill in Strawberry Point because April knew that her old friend would worry if she didn't hear from her soon. Before she would explain what had happened, she extracted a blood oath from Suze that she would not breathe a word of April's misadventures to anyone back home.

When she told her about Jake, the ever-optimistic Suze gushed in clichés about black clouds with silver linings and advised April not to be a babe in the woods, to keep a stiff upper lip, and not to look a gift horse in the mouth. April hung up with a promise to call again soon and went outside to join Jake and the girls for dinner on the patio. They'd talked him into driving them to a movie, so after a light supper, she and Jake dropped Molly and Staci off at a nearby theater.

Jake and April used the time for driving around town and scouting out potential business sites. None of them suited her as well as the Onion did, and she made up her mind to take Jake's advice and talk to Joe Castelli again ... once her other problems had been straightened out.

CHAPTER FIVE

AT HARRY TANNER'S barbecue the next day, Chaz took Jake aside and pounded him on the back. "Well, ole buddy, looks like you've met your match."

"April and I are just friends, *old* buddy." Jake didn't mention how he'd had to con her into coming with him by reminding her that it would be unpatriotic not to celebrate the Fourth, and downright un-American not to pay tribute to the team that had won big in the NBA play-offs.

She'd still had reservations that the outing seemed too much like a date, and he'd had to promise her that he wouldn't think of it in that way, that they'd both go as free agents. He turned his attention back to the buffet and resumed filling his plates.

"Um-hum. Hell, man, I was beginning to think you two were inseparable."

"Hardly. She's sitting over there talking and I'm way over here." And, damn it, she was talking to three of the worst wolves on the team, even worse than himself in his heyday. "We are not joined at the hip, or anywhere else for that matter."

"You've been knocking yourself out all afternoon to

make sure she's having a good time, and now you're fixing her plate," Chaz pointed out.

"I think Jake is being sweet. Leave him be, Chaz," Ivy chastised her husband. "You used to do those things for me, too. Remember?"

"That's my point, Ivy." Chaz deftly dodged the forthcoming elbow, wrapped one big bear's paw around his wife, and placed a loud smacking kiss on her mouth. As he guided her away, he said over his shoulder to Jake, "*You've* been hooked, old chum. Now all you have to do is reel *her* in."

Jake piled coleslaw, potato salad, and steaks on the plates and wondered if bringing April here had been a mistake. His matchmaker cum daughter had wangled an invitation for herself and Staci to go sailing with Mags' family, conveniently absenting themselves for the day. He'd known why she had done it and had acknowledged the ruse by telling Molly he owed her one.

He looked across the lawn to where April was sitting on a garden bench surrounded by his teammates. The way they were hanging on to her every word reminded him of the Scarlett-and-her-suitors scene in *Gone With the Wind*. The big phonies. Why didn't they get their own women? Hell, why wouldn't they be interested in her—she was pretty, intelligent, and sexy in a wholesome way. She was also great fun.

It took a few minutes for Jake to realize what was happening. He was jealous! It was an emotion he'd never had to deal with before and one he soon discovered he didn't like. He ignored the dessert table completely in his haste to return to her side.

At first April was bewildered when Jake's teammates converged on her; then she was flattered. Although she didn't need or want a man in her life, there was no harm in basking in the glow of so much admiration, even if it was insincere at best. Her self-confidence had grown with each flirtatious comment, and their flattery had fallen on her ears like rain on the arid desert of her womanhood.

When Jake returned with their plates, he trod heavily on the foot of the young rookie sitting next to her.

"Sorry, pal," he said in no uncertain terms, "but that's my chair."

The young man eyed Jake and then shrugged as if deciding not to challenge the remark. "See ya' around, April."

Jake thrust a heaping plate at her and sat down. He cut a chunk of steak, popped it into his mouth, chewed vigorously, swallowed, and sighed with dramatic ecstasy. "I heard through the grapevine that there aren't enough steaks to go around. Unless you guys want a burger, you'd better hightail it over to the grill right now."

The men nearly knocked over their chairs in their haste, and April thought Jake looked very smug. "Why did you do that?"

He looked up, as innocent as a newborn babe. "Do what?"

"Are they really out of steaks?"

"Anything's possible." Jake glanced away from her as Chaz and Ivy passed by. "Hey, you two, come and sit with us."

April had met the couple upon their arrival at the party and liked them immediately. Chaz was funny and outgoing, Ivy his more reserved counterpart.

Ivy inquired after Molly, and Jake explained how she had wangled an invitation for herself and Staci to spend the day sailing with Mags and Fred and the kids. He didn't mention that he owed Molly one.

They had just finished eating when two small boys ran up and breathlessly begged Jake and Chaz to play a game of horse with them.

"Aren't you guys a little short for a game of b-ball?" Jake teased.

When the boys giggled and told them not that kind of horse, the two tall men scooped the children onto their backs and galloped off whooping like renegades.

Ivy asked politely about Staci and how April liked Florida. The subject of basketball came up and Ivy told April about the recent championship. April listened and responded appropriately, but watched Jake from the corner of her eye, her forehead furrowed in confusion.

Was this the same Jake Keegan she'd heard and read so much about? A man who had sown enough wild oats to feed the free world? Who attracted women by the dozens and took them skiing in the Swiss Alps and swimming in the Bahamas?

At the restaurant on Saturday, he'd been humble and had quickly changed the subject when Joe had praised him for his many acts of kindness. Today he had been thoughtful and considerate and sweet. He even played games with his teammates' children and was liked and respected by all of them. He made her smile more than she had in years, and his kisses made her feel like a woman, desired and wanted.

Ivy noticed that April was having a hard time keeping her eyes off Jake. "Quite a guy, isn't he?"

"He is." April forced herself to look away.

"You sound worried," Ivy prompted.

"I am." April forced out a chuckle and explained all the events leading up to and including the past three days. "So here I am, stranded with an impressionable young daughter in the home of the notorious Jake the Rake. With no money and nowhere else to go."

"Jake won't give you any trouble. He doesn't have to force himself on women."

"I can believe that," April said with a frown. "But I think he's pretty confident that he won't have to."

Ivy grinned. "If he likes you and you like him, what's the problem?"

April glanced at Jake, whose antics had the children giggling. A hopeful young sweet thing with long raven hair had joined in and was flashing perfect white teeth at Jake.

Out of the Blue

A knot formed in April's stomach and she forced herself to look away.

"I'm worried that if I indulge in too much of a good thing, I'll end up with heartburn," she mused out loud.

"I thought the same thing about Chaz."

"Was he a ladies' man, too?"

"Honey, he's a man. Chaz still has his fair share of groupies hanging around, but my face is the one he searches for in the crowded bleachers."

"You don't worry about those other faces?"

"Not anymore." Ivy smiled fondly. "It took Chaz five minutes to proposition me in the supermarket. I'd never laid eyes on him before, so of course I declined."

"Of course."

"I'm strong-willed. I held out until the third date."

Both women laughed. Then April asked, "How many weeks? Two, three?"

"Three days." Ivy winked.

"That long?"

"I was in love, but I was scared to death. Chaz only went to his apartment for clean clothes after that. Two weeks later he begged me to move in with him, but I refused. That was our first fight. He slammed out of my apartment and went home."

"Obviously you two made up." April gestured at the large diamond Ivy sported.

"It wasn't so obvious at the time. My heart was broken, and I was sure he'd find another girl the next day, sure that he wouldn't even miss me."

"What happened? Did he cool off and come to his senses?"

"No, my Chaz can be mule-minded when he wants to be. He injured his knee a couple of months later in an exhibition game. He underwent laser surgery and had too much time on his hands while he was recuperating. The sweet things came and went, but Chaz was slowly going crazy. He finally figured out that he wanted more than a full-time bedmate, that he wanted someone he could talk to, laugh with, share his life with. In other words," Ivy paused and patted her hair for emphasis, "he wanted me."

"And that was that?"

"More or less. We eventually tied the knot, but it took him a whole year to get up enough nerve to propose. I held out until I was certain he could be domesticated."

"He certainly seems so now." April gestured at the pile-up of two big boys and several small ones.

"What about you?" Ivy asked. "What are your plans?"

"Me?"

"Jake will probably wring my neck for this, but you're welcome to come and stay with us," Ivy offered, then glanced up to see that the game was ending. "Uh-oh, here they come. If you want to move over to our place, just say the word. I'll do the deed."

"That's very kind of you, Ivy, but there's no need. It's just until tomorrow." For some reason, April had to see this thing through to its conclusion; besides, if she had held him off this long, she could last for one more night.

The rest of the afternoon was action-packed, and April couldn't remember ever having had so much fun in a single day. She and Jake did everything together. They participated in a rough version of water basketball, and April accused Jake of goal tending and dunked him. Jake called a foul and threatened her with paying the penalty. She was tempted to wait around and find out what he had in mind but left the pool instead, pleading exhaustion and hunger.

By the time they'd eaten another meal, dusk had descended. A band had set up at one end of the tennis court, and a short distance away, fireworks lit up the sky. Excited, laughing youngsters chased through the crowd waving sparklers. The magical wands in their tiny fists overflowed, splashing star-pointed sparks in all directions as they made tiny neon circles in the air.

Taking her by the hand, Jake pulled April into a secluded corner. Turning to her, their bodies only inches apart, he asked, "Will you dance with me?"

Heart hammering and eyes wide, she stared up at him. It was shocking to her that the promise of being held in his arms could make her forget her best intentions. She didn't want anyone to have that much power over her ever again.

"Here? Everyone else is dancing on the tennis court."

"I misplaced my shoes and socks somewhere and that concrete might be too much for me. I'm not as tough as I look, and I'm much too lazy and content to look for shoes right now." Jake reached for her hand but she backed away. He stepped forward. "You're scared."

"You flatter yourself if you think I'm afraid of you." She took two steps backward, then headed for the safety of the crowd.

He followed, mindless of his bare feet. "Not of me. It's fighting your own feelings that has you worried."

"I'm not worried at all." She wondered if she sounded convincing to him. She didn't convince herself. Damn him, why did he have to pick on her? There were hundreds of women out there who were perfectly willing to do anything he wanted. Why her? She dodged her way through the sparkler-waving youngsters, then turned abruptly, intending to go back and ask him that very question.

"I thought I was the Big Bad Wolf, but it looks like Little Red has her own ideas," he called after her. "Hey, I'm open to..." His words trailed away when he stepped on a cast-off sparkler. It was still hot, and a dreadful pain seared his foot.

"Ow, ow, ow...damn! Ooh, ooh, ooh!" He ranted and hopped about on one foot before plopping down in the soft grass, cradling his injured foot in his lap.

April ran to him when she heard his moaning. "What happened?" She sank to her knees and bent over him. Gently she brushed away bits of grass from his foot. "It's burned, but not badly. Let's ask Harry for something to put on it." She glanced up and their gazes locked.

Lost in the blue depths of her eyes, Jake forgot about the pain, forgot about the party, forgot everything. "Take me home," he whispered. He took her arm, and heaven only knew what might have happened next if Chaz hadn't walked up just then, a reminder that there were others present.

"Hey, ole buddy, what happened?" Chaz clapped him on the back.

"He burned his foot, Chaz. Help me get him to the car."

Jake put an arm around April's shoulders and she helped him stand. "It isn't that bad," he protested but kept his arm where it was. He hated to admit it, but he had thought about playing on her sympathy. Then, when he saw how worried and vulnerable she looked, he changed his mind. "I can walk. There's no reason for Chaz to leave the party."

"Are you sure?" April frowned up at him with concern.

"It's nothing," he said with a reassuring smile.

"I think he's right, April. It doesn't look too bad," Chaz agreed.

"Do you want to stay then?" April asked.

"No, I'd better go home and put something on it. It's beginning to hurt."

Jake asked Chaz to make their excuses and he let April drive home. She drove carefully but shaved a few minutes off the trip by nudging the speed limit. "Here we are," she said unnecessarily.

Jake nodded. "I'm tempted to kiss the ground, that's how relieved I am to get out of the car."

April jumped out and hurried to catch up with him as he limped up the walk. "I wasn't driving that fast."

"Oh, yeah? You should go on the circuit. You could give the pros a run for the money." Jake hobbled to the front door, punched in the combination for the burglar alarm, and unlocked it before turning back to her.

She ignored his sarcasm and followed him inside. "Sit down and I'll take care of that foot."

"I'm going to take a shower first; I'm hot."

"Bragging?" She couldn't believe her bravado and decided that it stemmed from the fact that the girls would be home soon. It was almost ten o'clock, the time that Jake's sister had promised to drop them off.

"Not this time," he replied, noting her sassy grin. "Just complaining." Jake disappeared into his room.

April took a quick shower and changed into a pink-cotton jumpsuit. She refused to think about tomorrow, when she and Staci would be leaving for good. Because that meant wondering whether or not she would ever see Jake again, and she couldn't bear the thought that she might not.

Jake showered and shaved and spritzed himself with the expensive cologne he'd endorsed last year. And he did it all in less than ten minutes. He laid out on the bedside table the items Dr. April might need for fixing up his foot and switched on the answering machine.

The first voice he heard was Molly's. "Hi, Pops, it's me. We're having so much fun," she began sarcastically, "that we decided to spend the night with Aunt Mags. She'll drop us off tomorrow afternoon. I hope you and April can find something to do without us. Remember one thing, Pops, I love you and it's for your own good. Whoops, that was two things, wasn't it?" Molly paused for breath, then with dramatic intensity continued, "Whatever you do, make my sacrifice count!"

Jake chuckled ruefully as he turned off the machine. That kid was too much. How would April take the news that the girls wouldn't be here to save her? From him? From herself? He reclined on the bed, artfully arranged his short robe, and called, "April! I'm ready."

Startled, April jumped back, her fist in mid knock. She took a deep breath and opened the door a crack. "How's the foot?" At the prospect of entering Jake's bedroom, she was acting like a trembly teenager, but the sight of him lying on his bed, dressed in a chocolate-brown robe the same color as his eyes, was enough to make anyone nervous.

"It hurts. I don't think I should walk on it, so I'll just go to bed."

April pressed her forehead against the door and wished the hollow-core wood was the only obstacle between them. "You should use the burn ointment."

"I'll be fine, it's nothing. Really."

"Well," she stalled, wishing he would at least try to convince her to come inside. "If you're sure."

"I'm sure." Jake slammed his hand against the nightstand in frustration, knocking the bandage tin to the floor.

She heard the clatter and threw open the door. "Are you all right? I heard something and . . ." With each word, she drew closer to the bed.

"I'm okay," he said with a sheepish grin. Then he went on, compounding the lie. "I was going to put a bandage on so I wouldn't hurt it during the night. When I was a kid, a bandage always made the boo-boo feel better."

"Is it painful?"

"A little." Jake was careful to add just the right amount of sincerity to his tone.

After careful inspection, April chose an ointment and sat down on the bed, taking his foot in her lap. He sighed when she gently smoothed the salve on his wound. "Did I hurt you?"

"Yes," he breathed, jerking his foot away. "But not the way you think."

It all happened so fast, she had no idea how she ended up sprawled beneath him on the bed, his hands cupping her face. Her self-control went up in smoke and her chest heaved as she asked, "Why are you doing this, Jake?"

He breathed heavily into her ear. "Because I like you and I think you like me. And frankly, my dear, it needs to be done."

"But we don't really know each other, and I'm not willing."

"Your body says otherwise."

"I'm not a slave to my impulses," she said breathlessly.

"Surely there are hundreds of bodies out there for you to choose from, willing and accomplished bodies."

"Nay, thousands," he teased.

"You could take your pick..."

He kissed her temples. "But I want the one that goes with these gorgeous eyes." He nipped her ear with his teeth. "And these perfect earlobes. Your earlobes drive me crazy, you know."

Responding in spite of herself, April halfheartedly dodged his next assault. "They do not," she argued.

"But they do. Why else would I walk on hot coals just to be alone with you?" He angled himself above her, his lips only inches from hers. "I had a different game of 'doctor' in mind when I stepped on that sparkler tonight."

She ducked under his arms and sat up. "Are you saying that you did it on purpose? You actually intended to burn yourself?"

"Hell, no. I didn't plan on getting burned at all. I must have done something wrong. Eastern fire-walkers do it all the time and never get so much as a blister." Jake sat up beside her and propped the injured foot on his other leg. "I guess my concentration was broken somewhere between placing my tender foot on the sparkler and the first big ouch."

April tried to forget how he could make her laugh and tried to cling to her irritation. "You manipulated me."

"Shamelessly." He took a deep breath. "I told you I couldn't be blamed for that. It's all your fault. I was tired of sharing you, I was desperate. And don't forget those gorgeous earlobes, they drive me wild. They do strange things to me, even as we speak," he said with a wink. "Come on, live dangerously, Red. Say you'll play nurse to my doctor."

April knew that she should be furious with him, but she smiled and allowed him to maneuver her against the pillows. Why did she feel so flattered? Why did she feel so happy? So womanly? Her limited experience with dating, both before her marriage and since Caleb's death, had left her unprepared for her response to Jake. Before, she'd felt as though she were cheating on her dead husband, but so far, with Jake, there had been no shameful guilt, no soul-searching—just honest-to-goodness pleasure. He made her forget the past and think about the future, and she wondered if that was a sign that she had completed the grieving process at last.

"Will you?" he asked, his words a breathy whisper against her ear, his body tense and waiting.

"What? Play doctor?" Her hands slid to his shoulders.

"Yes." He leaned back a bit to look into her eyes and his hands slid up to cup her breasts.

"I don't play games, Jake," she said meaningfully. "I hate to lose."

"Red, this game is rigged." He planted his lips on hers. "There are no losers."

She had never experienced such total abandonment in a single kiss. His mouth was warm and moist and knowing. He tasted so good that she dared to let her tongue dart between his lips for more. As the kiss deepened, Jake's hand curled around her neck, stroking, moving ever downward.

His roaming fingers lowered the zipper on her jumpsuit with agonizing slowness, and April knew she should push away before it was too late, but she couldn't; her arms were tightly clasped around his neck. She couldn't summon the resistance and her voice was a husky whisper against his lips.

"We should stop."

He gently nipped her bottom lip with his teeth and then rested his forehead against hers, breathing hard. His hand stilled. "Why would we want to do something dumb like that?" he asked breathlessly.

April knew there were many reasons, but it took several seconds for her to remember just one of them. "The girls, they'll be home soon. They could come in here at any minute."

"They won't." Jake's lips nibbled hers.

April allowed it. "They won't?"

"Molly called and said they were spending the night with Mags in St. Augustine." He nuzzled her neck as she fell back on the pillows. "We've got all night. They won't be back until tomorrow afternoon."

She needed a reason to call a halt, but any she dredged up seemed ridiculous. Maybe it was meant to be; maybe she needed the experience that a brief encounter with Jake would give her. She certainly wanted him badly enough. There was no reason she shouldn't have him, at least for the night.

"Will you kiss me again, Jake?"

"I'll do anything." He caught her bottom lip between his teeth and caressed it with his tongue, then released it to kiss her with soul-wrenching intensity.

She trembled with desire. She had never known that a man's body could be this appealing. She wanted to touch him, to discover every sensitive spot he possessed. Instead, her fingers gripped the lapels of his terry-cloth robe and held on for dear life.

Jake sensed April's acquiescence by her sensuous movements. She writhed beneath him, and desire for her throbbed in his loins and raced through his veins. He was no longer engineering what was happening between them, and a niggling voice told him that it would soon be too late to turn back.

"April," he gasped. He pried his lips from hers. He rolled from the bed.

"What?"

"I'm sorry, but if we do this much longer, I won't be able to stop."

"I'm not sure, but I may have changed my mind about that."

"Look, you said yourself that I could have dozens of

women. But I want you. I want a depth of intimacy that two people rarely find, and I think that together we could have it. It has to be more than sex—I want that for us, too—but I want it all in good time. I want to prove to you that I'm not just on the make, and one way of doing that is by following convention, by having the courtship first."

April didn't speak. What could she say? She'd been rejected at the last moment. Should she take it personally, his choosing her to practice propriety on?

He got up and paced the floor. "I don't want to mess this up. It's too important for that. Do you understand?"

"Of course," she lied, easing herself from the bed. She held her head high and marched to the door.

He called to her softly, "Please don't be mad at me, Red."

"I'm not mad, I'm bewildered. But then, there's nothing new about that. I've been bewildered since I met you."

He went to her and took her hands and refused to release them when she tried to pull away. "I know that we just met and that you don't trust me yet. I don't understand what's happening here, but something is. Let's give it a chance. I think we can be more than simple chemistry to each other. Won't you let me test my theory?" He pulled her closer and she didn't resist.

Instead, she sighed and allowed Jake to wrap his arms around her. He buried his face in her neck as her arms went around him. Then his lips covered hers gently and a multitude of brand-new emotions tangled within her. She didn't know what to think, nor did she know what to do.

"I knew I wasn't ready for you," she whispered.

CHAPTER SIX

APRIL LAY AWAKE for a long time after leaving Jake's arms to go to her own room. He'd been so sweet and sincere when he turned her away that instead of being angry, she had been almost flattered. If she had had doubts earlier that his interest was genuine, she didn't now. That's what made the situation so impossible.

Even though it was something she'd never done before, indulging in a casual affair was preferable to getting involved in a relationship at this point in her life. She just didn't have the time to devote to it. As attractive as she found Jake, they were two very different people, with little except daughters in common. Her heated response to him, she kept reminding herself, was simply the result of long-denied needs.

With that thought, she fell into a restless sleep. When she awakened the next morning, her internal debate picked up right where it had left off. Maybe she should have gone back to his room and seduced him. But that idea raised another problem. How did a lady go about seducing a man and still remain a lady? Damn him anyway! He was Jake the Rake, and she had been willing to give in to passion, so why had she slept alone last night?

Determined not to let the problem detract from her enjoyment of the new day, she hurried out of bed and into the shower. She would have money wire-transferred from home to a new checking account here in Jacksonville and get some blessed cash. Having money meant that she could repay Jake and be out of his debt. Money meant that she and Staci could move into a motel. Money meant freedom and independence, and she'd felt helpless long enough.

She dressed quickly and bounded down the stairs. Hesitating at the kitchen door, April squared her shoulders and gave herself some advice. She would act as though nothing had happened last night, because after all, nothing had. She would be pleasant, drink a little coffee, then call Ivy and ask for transportation to the nearest branch of her bank. What could be simpler? Yes indeed, things were looking up.

The telephone rang just as she stepped into the kitchen. She walked over to the stove where Jake was frying eggs and held out her hand for the spatula. "I'll watch the eggs while you get the phone," she offered.

"First things first." His grin was lopsided as he leaned over to brush his lips across hers. "Good morning, Red."

Every nerve ending in her body tingled, and April knew she was a goner. Better get those plans underway as soon as possible. "Good morning, yourself."

"Hungry?" The phone continued to ring as he dished up the eggs and set the plates on the bar where they sat side by side.

"Aren't you going to answer that?"

"No, that's what answering machines are for." He passed her the orange marmalade, propped his elbows on the bar, and watched as she spread it on her toast.

His approving gaze unnerved her and she attempted to fill the void with conversation. "What if it's Molly? What if she needs you?"

Jake reached over and tucked a strand of hair behind her

ear. "I can hear the caller when he leaves the message. If it's important, I'll pick up the receiver."

It was pretty early in the morning for his eyes to be so bold and seductive, and entirely too early for her unbidden response to their sensuous glint. But how could she fail to notice his hair, damp and touseled from his shower? Or the fresh citrusy scent of his after-shave? She spied a fleck of overlooked shaving cream on his ear, and without thinking, she reached out to wipe it away. His eyes widened and he leaned into her touch as if welcoming it. What had been meant as an innocent gesture jolted her into even deeper awareness of him.

Caught up in her thoughts, April missed most of the message being left on the recorder. It was a good thing she would be leaving his house today; her heart threatened to become as involved as her body already had.

Jake picked up the phone and handed it to her. "It's for you."

"Hello? Yes, this is April Conway. An apartment is available after all? Oh, yes, I do still want it . . . fine . . . I'll be there today. Thank you. Good-bye."

April hung up and summoned more enthusiasm than she felt before turning to Jake. "Good news. Mrs. Grodin from the real-estate office says she has an apartment for us. It's a bit smaller than the one I originally leased, but we can move in whenever we want to—today, in fact. Isn't that wonderful?"

"Yeah, swell," he mumbled, pretending a sudden interest in buttering his toast. "Today?"

"Yes. She said she'd call back in a few moments with the directions."

"If you don't like it, or if it's in a bad neighborhood, don't feel you have to take it." Jake didn't like the idea of April moving out so soon, and he clutched at any tiny straw of hope.

They tried to finish eating, but neither of them seemed

to have much appetite. Without further conversation, they began to clear away the clutter.

The task soon became April's alone. Jake answered one call after another, and she decided that he must be a popular date indeed if the number of mumbled, "sorry-but-I'm-sort-of-tied-up-at-the-moment" replies were any indication. Three times he answered the phone, turned his back, and made that statement while April crammed plates, glasses, and flatware into the dishwasher with little regard for potential breakage.

When the phone rang a fourth time, she gave the door of the dishwasher an angry shove and it closed noisily. She yanked off a paper towel, dried her hands, and turned to leave him to his girl-tending in solitude.

"April," Jake called, "it's for you." Before handing her the receiver, he gave her a cautious reminder. "Don't say yes until we've seen it."

By the time she hung up, she knew her luck had changed. It wasn't Mrs. Grodin, but a representative of the moving company. They had located her household goods and were terribly sorry for any inconvenience they'd caused her. To make it up to her, they wouldn't charge her for storage. When she tentatively asked if they might be able to deliver her things today, the company official assured her they could.

Things progressed so quickly that by the time the girls came home and were hustled into Jake's car, all the arrangements had been made. After a detour by the bank, where April was duly fawned over because she was in the exalted presence of Jake Keegan, they arrived at the new apartment.

It was a modest enough place, but April fell in love with it the moment she saw it. The walls were white, the carpet silver-gray. Abundant windows let in the sunshine, and white ceiling fans whirred overhead. April had elected not to move any furniture with her—most of it belonged to the Conways anyway—and so had rented the apartment furnished. The living-room couch and chairs were upholstered in a muted gray-and-white striped fabric, and the tables were finished in shiny black lacquer. The kitchen was small but bright, and there were two striped bar stools at the counter dividing the living room from the dining area.

Despite Jake's grumbling that she was paying too much for it, April knew that she and Staci could be happy here. There was a small patio in back, and a little privacy-fenced yard where they could sit out in the evenings. She had been warmly welcomed by the resident managers, a friendly, capable retired couple who told her to let them know if she needed anything. Yes, her prospects were definitely beginning to look brighter.

Staci hadn't been too happy when she returned from St. Augustine to discover that they were moving, but she had been soothed by Molly's assurances that they would go to the same school and could visit often as well as talk to each other on the phone every day. After their initial exploration of the new apartment, the two were sent to Staci's bedroom to instruct the movers where to place her things.

A beefy-looking man struggled in with a box labeled "S Bedroom" and snapped, "Where to, lady?"

His surly attitude left April momentarily at a loss for words.

"Come on, we ain't got all day." He dropped the box to the floor with a thud.

Jake had been checking out the tiny kitchen but entered the hall a second later. He walked up behind April and hooked a possessive hand over her shoulder. "What's the problem here?"

"Hey, ain't you Jake Keegan?" The man held out his right hand and Jake obliged him by shaking it. "Call me Bernie, and hey," he gushed, still pumping Jake's hand, "that was one helluva championship game. How's it feel to be voted the league's MVP?"

Without giving Jake time to answer, Bernie turned to two men coming up the sidewalk lugging a heavy wardrobe box. "Julio, Paul, hurry up with that, and be careful not to damage any of Mr. Keegan's stuff while you're at it." He hefted his box and turned to April with a beaming smile. His voice was almost humble when he asked, "Where would you like this to go, ma'am?"

Only the need to have her belongings prevented April from telling Bernie what he could do with the whole truckload. Then she reconsidered. As far as she could tell, Bernie's awestruck behavior was fairly typical of the local sports fans.

She encouraged Jake to go, telling him that she and Staci were grateful but they couldn't possibly ask him to help them unpack. He shook his head firmly and told her they were friends and that one needn't ask anything of a friend.

The movers, spurred on by the chance to do a favor for Jake the Rake, worked like dynamos. They had everything off the truck and into its proper room in the apartment within a couple of hours. They accepted glasses of iced tea and talked basketball while April wrote them a check that Jake had already verbally endorsed.

Later, as the foursome unpacked boxes and put away kitchen items, Staci stood up and crossed her arms, her expression mutinous. "I'm not doing any more work until you feed me. We haven't had a bite since brunch, and I'm starving."

Molly copied her actions. "Me, too."

"A bite?" Jake's hands became claws, and in a stumbling gait he advanced on the squealing girls. "I haf come all the vay from Transylvania to gif you a bite."

April laughed as they ran screaming from the room and Jake hobbled after them. The three ended up on the living-room floor in a free-for-all that had Jake begging for mercy and April wishing she were part of it. The girls continued to tickle him until he promised to take them to the River Walk for a seafood dinner.

Their non-dates were mostly conducted in restaurants,

and April found a kind of comfort in the fact that if Jake kept insisting on feeding her, she'd gain enough weight to quell his interest entirely. Still, when the lobster was served, she declined the drawn butter.

The food was fabulous, and April secretly enjoyed the fact that the waitress assumed they were a family. For a reason she didn't fully understand, she was also pleased that Jake didn't bother to enlighten the young woman.

The sights were not to be missed, and Jake was a delightful tour guide. Live bands performed up and down the boardwalk, and they took a water taxi across the St. John's River for a quick look in Orange Park Mall. He bought all of them matching T-shirts decorated with the state's most famous fruit and reading "Orange you glad you live in Florida?"

Because everyone was tired, they agreed to call it an early evening. When Jake dropped April and Staci off at the apartment, he didn't say when he would see them again, but first thing the next morning, the Keegans showed up at the apartment sporting their new T-shirts.

"Get your shirts on," Jake instructed, "and we'll go out for breakfast. Then I'll introduce you to my favorite market so you can stock up on groceries."

"You don't have to go to so much trouble," April protested. As much as she enjoyed his company, she had reservations about falling into a situation where he took it for granted that she'd spend all her time with him.

"You have to eat, and since you don't have a car yet, you need transportation. Right?"

He had her there. She sent out a prayer that the police would recover the Bronco soon.

At the supermarket, Molly spied a couple of her friends in the bakery section and hurried Staci over to meet them. The grown-ups knew when they weren't needed; they didn't have to be particularly astute to understand Molly's what-are-you-waiting-for tone as she called out to them, "Go ahead, we'll catch up later."

"I'll push the cart, you load," Jake insisted.

"I like to push and load," April told him. "I've done it for years."

"I know that, Red." He sighed. "It's just that I'll feel like excess baggage if I don't do something. But if it's too threatening to your independence, I'll follow along behind like a faithful little puppy dog."

"Okay, you win." She smiled ruefully. "I admit I can be a bit touchy on the subject of doing things my way, but if it means that much, then you may push the cart, Jake."

He was about to make a smart remark when he glanced over her shoulder and spotted the last person in the world he wanted to see. They were caught, and there was no place to hide. "Oh, no," he groaned as a woman's strident voice assaulted them. "Jake? Jake Keegan, you devil, is that really you?"

April embraced a box of detergent and watched as Jake sped off with the cart. He yanked the mirror-lensed glasses from the top of his head and covered his eyes. "Let's go," he hissed to April over his shoulder.

"Jake! Come back here, Jake." The woman breezed by April, caught up to him, and grabbed his hand. "My Gawd, you look like a tourist," she exclaimed as she threw her arms around him, hugging him with abandon. She leaned back from the waist and winked at him. "Long time no see, no call. I almost didn't recognize you."

"That would have been too bad, Gretchen." Jake firmly set her aside and held out his hand to April, his eyes pleading with her to understand that this wasn't his idea. "April?"

She plunked the detergent into the cart and waited, refusing to take his hand. He introduced the two women, who made it clear they had no desire to meet.

April studied the brunette to see if she could uncover some redeeming feature she might have missed. Nope. There didn't seem to be any. She was attractive in an artificial way, suggesting that a couple of unpleasing features might have been adjusted to suit her. Her strapless sundress revealed a lot of darkly tanned skin, and April derived pleasure from the fact that in ten years, the woman would look like she was constructed of Portuguese leather.

"Wherever did you meet her, Jakie?" Gretchen asked in a tone insinuating that such a mismatched alliance must be accidental and surely wouldn't last long. Then the brunette pouted prettily at Jake and gently raked one of her blood-red nails down the exposed length of his forearm.

"He picked me up at the police station." April hated to think that this was the kind of woman Jake was partial to. She wasn't sure that the snide female had any curiosity, but if she did, that little comment should spark it.

"Oh, Jakie, you really shouldn't do that sort of thing, dear. I know how titillating the forbidden can be, but you never know where that sort has been."

April pretended to misunderstand the contemptuous remark. "I recently moved here from Iowa."

Jake bit his lip to keep from grinning and tried to change the subject. "How about the new bakery here? Sure smells great. Molly stopped off over there first thing."

"Molly? There are two of them?" Gretchen frowned at him. "And to think I always thought you too inhibited for my tastes. Silly me! Is this Molly creature anything like *her*?"

Gretchen was pushing Jake's limits of common courtesy, and if she didn't shut up and move on soon, he might just have to tell her where to take her unjustified jealousy and tasteless remarks. "She might be when she grows up, if I'm lucky."

Jake saw the triumphant smile on Gretchen's face and wondered what she thought she knew. He wouldn't put anything past her and couldn't understand why he had ever asked her out in the first place. He watched her expression turn sly at his next statement.

"We really should find Molly and Staci now." Taking April by the arm with one hand and pushing the cart with the other, he said over his shoulder, "So long, Gretchen."

"Three!" Gretchen clapped her hands excitedly. "Hey, Jakie, I'll give you a call."

"Please don't. I really have my hands full."

They had barely rounded the corner when April turned on him. "Do you realize what she was thinking?"

He grinned. "Even though I know her only slightly, I have a pretty good idea. People like Gretchen believe what they want to believe."

April said nothing but grabbed a can of green beans from the shelf and without warning, tossed it in his direction. "Heads up."

He deftly caught it, slam-dunking it into the grocery cart. With a chuckle, he bragged, "Good save, don't you think?"

"Probably. But it depends on the point of view. Yours," she said in a sarcastic aside, "or the eggs'?" April pointed out the gooey yellow mess oozing from the cart to form a slimy puddle on the gray-tiled floor.

Jake left her there laughing while he went in search of help. The cashier told him she would find someone to clean it up and drawled over the loudspeaker, "Jimmy, cleanup, please. Cleanup on aisle five." There was a pause, and then, "Make that heavy-duty, Jimmy."

"The clerk makes it sound like poor Jimmy might catch something by cleaning up our little accident," Jake said when he returned to April's side.

"*Our* little accident? You can leave me out of it." She wasn't sure if she was laughing because of the look on Gretchen's face when she'd assumed that Jake might have some perversions after all, or because of the look on Jake's face when he learned he had clobbered the eggs. He glared at her, but since his own sense of humor was so well-honed, he began laughing, too.

They were still giggling when they heard the cleanup detail coming. When Jimmy appeared, their hilarity doubled. The heavy-set, pink-faced young man pushed a big mop bucket on squeaky wheels. He wore a green rubber apron down to his shoe tops, and matching rubber gloves. An economy-sized squirt bottle hung in a holster on his hip, sloshing with each step he took, and a giant roll of paper towels was secured by a strap to the front of the apron.

"Sorry to take you away from your toxic waste disposal duties, Jimmy," Jake said seriously.

Jimmy grimaced, wrinkling his nose when he saw the mess. "Yucko."

"I'm sorry," April spluttered, battling for control.

"It was all my fault," Jake added, barely managing to tamp down another spurt of laughter.

Jimmy stared at him for a moment, and then his face lit up with recognition. "No problem, Jake. Think nothing of it." He grinned sheepishly and added, "Just as long as you made that basket. Right? Tell you what, why don't I just get another cart and replace these groceries with fresh ones? How about that?"

"You don't need to go to that much trouble," Jake protested.

"It'd be my pleasure." The kid beamed up at him. "Nothing's too good for the Rake!"

Everyone in Jacksonville, it seemed, was a sports fan. April glanced at Jake and rolled her eyes for his benefit. She had to wonder how he maintained any humility at all in the face of such virulent hero-worship.

The new telephone, which Jake had used his influence to acquire for her, was ringing when April unlocked the door. "It's probably a wrong number," she said with a chuckle, rushing to answer it while Jake and the girls carried in the groceries.

"Who was it?" Jake asked when he saw her face as she came into the living room. "Your in-laws?"

"No," she said, taking a deep breath. "I called them last night. Dad wanted to know all about our new place, and

Hazel sounded downright warm for a change. I don't understand it, but they seem to be accepting the fact that maybe I can take care of us after all."

"I understand it and I've never met the people."

"Oh, is that so? Pray tell us your analysis, Dr. Keegan."

"They've probably realized the truth in the old saying: If you can't fight 'em, join 'em."

Jake was right. Although she'd had no intention of stepping out of their lives, the Conways didn't know that. She'd tried to assure them that they would always be her family and Staci's, and she had realized that their insecurity was part of their reluctance to let her go. It would be difficult for them to accept that she had a life apart from them, but maybe in time, a complete reconciliation would be possible.

Jake interrupted her thoughts and asked again why the call had upset her.

"It was the police. Seems they found our car, or what's left of it. It was stripped before being burned and abandoned. The insurance will pay, but I'll have to go shopping for a new one."

"That won't be so bad. Buying a new car can be fun."

She frowned. "Only if you know what you're doing."

"I know a little something about cars, and I have a few contacts. Want some company?"

"Thanks, I'd appreciate it."

For several days, Jake delayed the car-buying trip in order to postpone the inevitable. Once April had a car, he would be obsolete and would have to think up much more creative reasons to see her. But since a promise was a promise, he took her around to the local dealerships until she found what she wanted. The dealer, star of his own Fred Phariss Ford TV commercials, was an ex-jock and a long-time friend and he offered April a deal on a Mustang convertible that she couldn't refuse. He didn't have a red one in stock, but he promised her that the cars he had on order would arrive in a couple of weeks.

"Not to worry, Mrs. Conway. I'll give you a demo to drive until then," Fred quickly reassured her, plucking a set of keys from the rack behind his desk. "Take the dark-blue convertible over there. Might as well enjoy the sunshine while you're waiting."

April accepted the keys. "That's really very kind of you. It will be nice to be mobile again. Thanks."

"Hey, any time," Fred said magnanimously. "Any friend of Jake's is a friend of mine."

They went outside and Jake was reluctant to let her drive away. He knew he didn't have the right to expect anything from her and that from here on out, she was a free agent. She had her own place, and she had her own wheels. She was no longer dependent on him, and he feared that she would begin distancing herself. His only hope was to delay the process for as long as possible.

"Why don't we pick up the girls and go out for dinner?" he suggested hopefully.

Going out to eat had become such a joke between them that April puffed out her cheeks to show her disdain for the idea. "Jake, I'm grateful for all your help. Very much so, but I don't want to go back to depending on a man for everything. How can I ever achieve autonomy as long as you're around? You cast too large a shadow."

"Okay, then we won't go out until the sun sets," he teased.

April sighed. "Okay, we'll eat together," she conceded. It wasn't much of a sacrifice. She had grown used to having him around and knew that she'd miss him if he weren't. He never failed to make her laugh, and as hard as it was to admit, she needed those sly glances and stolen kisses when the girls weren't looking.

"But, Jake?"

"Yes?"

"You do realize that I could have bought that car without you? Oh, maybe not for that price and without the added convenience of the demo, but I could have done it by myself."

"What are you getting at, Red?"

"That I don't need anyone to help me."

"I know that. You're the only one who doesn't believe it." Jake grinned and shook his head. "It's okay to be independent, but you have to learn that everybody needs somebody sometime. I just want to be the body you need."

CHAPTER SEVEN

WITH HER PERSONAL life once more in some semblance of order, April was finally free to pursue her professional goal. On a muggy afternoon in late July, she slipped into a booth at the Big Onion. She waved a cheery greeting to Joe Castelli, who left his customary spot behind the bar to come over and sit down across from her.

"How're you doing, Mrs. Conway?" he asked amiably. "What can I get you?"

Policy-wise, April believed in the importance of honesty. "What I really want is the deed to this place." She smiled at his surprised look and added, "But I'll settle for a bacon cheeseburger and a cherry Coke."

"Then you were serious when you made me that offer?" Joe scribbled her order on a pad and flagged down a passing waiter.

"As serious as a person can be. If you'll reconsider, I think I can make it worth your while."

"Jake told me I'd be hearing from you. So, you two are going to be partners then?"

She sighed. Joe seemed as intent as the rest of the world on teaming her up with Jake Keegan. The inference that she couldn't succeed on her own made her even more determined to prove she could. "No. Buying the restaurant is my own venture." She told him of her plans and explained why the Onion was a perfect location for what she wanted to do. Then she restated her offer, assuring him that she'd done her homework and knew it was a liberal price. She meant for him to get a fair deal. Propping her chin on one hand and leaning forward on her elbow, she asked, "What do you say, Joe?"

He scratched his chin and gazed thoughtfully out the window. "I say, let me sleep on it. You've made me an interesting offer and I want to give it some thought. Selling this place to anyone but Jake will be like cutting off a leg, but then again, it would be nice to get out of the rat race. You sure you know what you're getting into? Long hours, no days off, not even holidays."

"I know the limitations. And to tell you the truth, I welcome the challenge."

"I sure would like to retire before I get too old to enjoy the time off," Joe mused. "I've had my eye on a little bait-and-tackle shop out in Jacksonville Beach. A man could have a dandy retirement there."

"All the more reason for you to accept my offer." She knew he wanted to sell, but he seemed reluctant to make a commitment. Before she could give him another dozen reasons why he should accept her offer, her order arrived and he stood up.

"I'll leave you to eat in peace and you leave me to think in the same. I'll call you tomorrow with my decision. Deal?"

She said "I certainly hope so" over a firm handshake and Joe disappeared into the kitchen.

She ate her burger thoughtfully, speculating on whether or not she had convinced him. She could only hope that the lure of retiring in the sunshine would make him see things her way.

Glancing around, April visualized the changes she would make once the Onion belonged to her. Because she wanted to put her own stamp on the restaurant, she would begin by changing the name. To what, she didn't know yet, but she wanted a name that would reflect her concept of the place as well as its new look and mood, which would be gained by converting the "corner pub" ambience into that of a neighborhood bistro.

She'd start with a kelly-green-and-mauve color scheme for chic and add baskets of hanging plants to brighten up the dark interior. Subdued lighting and a new black-and-white checkerboard floor would lend a European flavor, as would the cloth-topped round tables that would replace the worn vinyl booths. She hoped to make arrangements with local artists for the display of their pastel and watercolor pictures, so that an ever-changing gallery of delicate artwork would adorn the pale mauve walls.

Knowing that it was premature to plan expansions before Joe had even accepted her offer, April couldn't help but imagine a much-needed addition. Since the restaurant was situated on a pie-shaped lot, there was plenty of room in which to add an alfresco dining area by constructing a walled-in terrace, complete with umbrella-topped tables and decorative greenery. With daily temperatures in the subtropical climate averaging seventy-three degrees, the landscaping potential was limitless, and she could almost see the mini-garden now, filled with the heavy scent of tropical flowers.

The fantasy had to become a reality, and April knew she could make it happen. Establishing and nurturing a business of her own was a dream she'd cherished for a long time, one she needed as much as wanted. Already she could see the place filled with satisfied customers who, by word of mouth alone, would ensure its success. If only Joe would agree to sell to her. If only she could acquire the necessary financing. If only luck would be on her side. That was a lot of "ifs," and April forced herself out of her reverie before she let them get her down.

She gestured for the waiter to bring her check. When he

told her it had been taken care of, she mouthed her thanks to Joe, who had resettled himself behind the bar. He dismissed her with an "it's nothing" wave and she left, hoping that his generosity was a good omen for their future business dealings.

She picked up Staci and Molly from their snorkeling lesson, and they described, in breathless detail, the "gorgeous hunk" who was their teacher. What they failed to mention was the underwater spectacle that had made them beg for the lessons in the first place. They had grown closer with each passing day, and the friendship had been good for both of them. Staci was overcoming some of her natural shyness, and Molly was beginning to act more like the child she was.

April waited at the curb until Molly was safely inside the house, but before she could pull away, Jake came bounding down the walk. Crouching low, he folded his arms on the window frame and grinned. "What are you doing later? One of my friends is having a party tonight and I'd like you to go with me."

She leaned slightly away from him, to put physical as well as emotional distance between them. Jake was persistent when it came to invitations. It was hard to resist some of his imaginative suggestions, but so far she'd turned them all down.

"I don't think so, Jake." Attending another party with his friends would mark them as a couple.

"If you don't like that idea, how about dancing?"

Dancing would be far too close for comfort. "Not tonight."

"A movie?"

"It's too late to find a sitter, and this is Conchata's night off." April had been relieved to meet the vivacious housekeeper when the woman returned to work earlier in the week. The middle-aged Conchata was offbeat to say the least, but she loved Jake and Molly as if they were her own family. "Sorry."

God, but the woman could be stubborn. Jake had hoped to wear her down before this. The relationship he had been so very eager to protect was in serious jeopardy of fizzling out completely. The longer things went on as they were, the easier it was for her to keep him at arm's length. Friendship! Who needed it?

"How about a walk on the beach? We can lock the kids in the car."

"That sounds like the suggestion of a desperate man."

To confirm her appraisal, he clamped his hands together in a gesture of supplication. "I'm begging you, Red. I need some friendly company."

"If ever a person had plenty of friends, you do. Call one of them."

She was practically insisting he take out another woman. Was that what she wanted? He had bowed to her ban on their dating by including the girls in their outings and by insisting that there were no prohibitions against friends sharing a meal, but that didn't make being with him any less dangerous. He hadn't overstepped the bounds of friendship since the night of the sparkler incident, and frankly, she was a tad disappointed, as well as suspicious of his motives.

As long as he actively pursued her, evading him was a cinch. But now that he had done a complete about-face, she was no longer sure of how to proceed. Maybe she had become less desirable to him, but he certainly hadn't lost any of his appeal for her, and she would be crazy to set herself up for more psychological stress. Perversely, his lack of physical aggression made her want him more, and the casual familiarity of being "just friends" was becoming impossible to tolerate.

When she was with him, she worried that they were spending too much time together, and when they were apart, she worried that he was spending time with someone else. She couldn't bear to think of him in the embrace of one of the whiskey-voiced women who left messages on his answering machine any more than she could bear spending another frustrating moment in his company but not in his arms.

"I don't want to call anyone else," he pouted.

"Thanks for thinking of me, but Staci and I have a quiet evening at home planned. I promised to give her a sewing lesson tonight. We're making tote bags."

"Sounds like fun." Jake tried to keep his tone light, but it wasn't easy. "Some other time."

April felt herself weakening and tried to be firm. "I need to spend time with Staci. I hope you understand."

"Sure, no problem." He didn't want to rush her, but if he left it up to her, their relationship would never get off the ground. He had given her the space she had asked for, and now it loomed between them like the Grand Canyon. Promises, hastily given, were sometimes hard to keep.

Changing the subject, April told him about her encouraging meeting with Joe. "I think he'll go for my offer. At least I hope so. I know it's silly, but I've been planning the new color scheme."

Jake noted the glow on her face when she spoke of her future business. He didn't want to discourage her, but he felt compelled to ask, "Do you have the financing lined up?"

Some of the glow disappeared. "Not yet. But I'm sure it won't be a problem. I haven't come this far just to let a trivial matter like money get in the way."

He straightened up. "Of course not. I'm sure you're right." But he wasn't. The only thing he was sure of was that April was going to get a shot at her dream. One way or another.

Joe called the next morning, and when she hung up, April couldn't stop dancing around the apartment.

"What is it, Mom?" Staci implored as her mother waltzed her about in happy circles. "Did we win a sweepstakes or something?"

"Better than that." April paused so that her next words would have the desired dramatic effect. "That was Mr. Castelli on the phone. He has agreed to sell me the Onion."

Staci's reaction proved she knew just how much the sale meant to her mother. "Really? You mean we're finally going to see our name on the five-star list?"

April hugged her daughter. "Maybe. But first I have to see our name on a loan contract. Hurry up and change clothes while I call the bank for an appointment."

"Since I don't have any dress-for-success outfits, will my blue sundress do?" Staci asked with an impish grin.

"It will do just fine. We're going to have those bankers eating out of our hands."

"I'd settle for having them eat in our restaurant," Staci tossed back.

April's confidence and bravado began to flag midway through her afternoon meeting with the bank's loan officer, Mr. Clarke. She'd gone to the bank fully prepared with carefully penciled spreadsheets indicating the cost of planned improvements. She'd stopped by Joe's to pick up a detailed report of the restaurant's income for the past five years, and she also had a projection of future income based on the increased traffic the improvements would engender.

She presented, verbally and on paper, her concept of the restaurant and why she knew it would succeed when others had failed, pointing out that it was already established in a proven location. She offered the officer her bank book as evidence that she had enough money in her personal account to see her through the first year, which was more than most would-be entrepreneurs could boast, and then she rested her case.

Mr. Clarke's expressions, which ranged from doubtful to downright discouraging, were enough to chill her enthusiasm. For the first time, she acknowledged failure as a possibility and felt a hollowness inside that she hadn't known since meeting Jake. She glanced at the banker and found him watching her instead of reading the projections she had presented.

In no way was she going to allow this smug man to sabotage her plans. However, he could certainly provide an unwanted setback. She had done everything possible to sell herself and the package; all she could do now was to await his decision.

The banker leaned back in his plush chair, steepled his fingers over his chest, and smiled patronizingly. "Mrs. Conway," he began, "I must say I'm impressed by your plans, and your enthusiasm certainly leaves nothing to be desired . . ."

"But?" she prompted coolly, resenting the fact that he was obviously trying to let her down easily with false flattery.

"But I have to question your lack of experience. You really know nothing of business in general or of the restaurant business in particular."

April felt a sudden rush of anger and tamped it down. A show of emotion was just what the man wanted. Sometime during the conversation, she had realized that he wasn't taking her seriously, because she was a woman. Hadn't the man even looked at her presentation? Did he think it the work of someone who knew nothing of business? Somehow she would have to change his closed mind.

"That's not true, Mr. Clarke. I worked closely with my husband in the family's dairy operation for years, and I understand cash flow, as well as the problems the lack of it can cause. I know the tax laws as they pertain to the small business, and I'm intimately acquainted with all areas of accounts payable. I know how to manage on a limited budget, and I don't expect to get rich quickly. It will take time for the restaurant to show a profit, but when looking at an undertaking such as this, one must be concerned with the long run, Mr. Clarke, not the short run. Don't you agree?"

He smiled again, but this time not with his eyes. "I must be concerned with the bank's investment, Mrs. Conway. I appreciate your experience, but a rural enterprise such as a dairy farm has very little in common with a big-city restaurant operation, which just happens to be one of the riskiest business ventures you could undertake. I seriously question your ability to succeed alone in this area."

She steepled *her* fingers. "So you've already made your decision?"

The man looked uncomfortable under April's blue gaze. "Of course not. I'll take your proposal before the loan committee. After all, you're a valuable customer, Mrs. Conway."

"But *you've* already made *your* decision," she insisted.

"We both know what that must be, don't we?" He shuffled the papers back into her portfolio. "To offer some hope, may I suggest that you find a partner who knows Jacksonville? Someone with either business experience or a business education. Someone willing to underwrite some of your expenses and co-sign the note. Have you considered such a possibility?"

"No, but just about everyone else has."

Checking her anger again, April was careful not to challenge the heart of the man's objection, which was, obviously, that as a woman, she could not succeed without the help of another person, preferably a man. No, she wouldn't let him know that she had correctly interpreted his unspoken signals. She wouldn't give him the satisfaction.

"I beg your pardon, Mrs. Conway?" The banker rose and slid her presentation across his desk.

"Never mind." She gathered the leather slipcase under her arm and crossed the room, knowing full well that for him the matter was closed. At the door she turned. "When will I know the loan committee's decision, Mr. Clarke?"

The man looked startled, as though he thought she already knew. "Why, as soon as I do, Mrs. Conway. As soon as I do."

Determined not to let her disappointment get her down, April invited Jake and Molly over that night. She could tell herself not to let Jake become important in her life, but at moments like this, it was obvious that she needed the comfort he so generously offered. She didn't want a shoulder to cry on, but she needed a sympathetic soul to commiserate with her.

"Buck up, kid," Jake cajoled after she recounted her meeting with the banker. "It's not the only bank in town."

She looked up from the salad she was tossing. "No, but I've done business with a branch of that bank for over ten years. If they won't trust me with a loan, who will?"

"I'm sure it has nothing to do with trust, Red." He snitched a cucumber slice from the salad bowl and munched it noisily. "If they turn you down, it'll be for purely business reasons. Money's tight right now."

"Isn't it always?" She vented her frustration on the hapless greens, determined not to feel sorry for herself.

"Did the bank suggest an alternative financing plan?"

She crumbled bacon into the salad and threw in a handful of croutons. "If that's what you want to call it. Clarke told me to find a rich partner who knew Jacksonville and would be willing to co-sign." She looked up to find Jake grinning.

"Hey, look no farther."

"Thanks, but I—"

"You want to do this yourself," he chanted.

"That's right."

April's tone was cheerful, but she had begun to doubt her ability to go it alone. She slid an aromatic pan of lasagne out of the oven and called everyone to the table. In the familial atmosphere that ensued, business was forgotten and she marveled at Jake's ability to take her mind off pressing matters. His silly jokes made her laugh, and the girls giggled and joined in.

Later, he helped with the dishes, and April couldn't help thinking how nice he would be to come home to, how comforting his presence would be in times of trouble. It had been a long time since she had felt so safe and comfortable with a man, and it was wonderful to once again have someone to talk to.

Jake could make her laugh when all she felt like doing was crying. He made her believe in herself because he believed in her. He kept her from taking herself too seriously, and accepted what she had to give without demanding more.

Companionably, they sat on the couch in April's darkened living room and watched an old movie on television. The girls had long since retreated to Staci's room, complaining about black-and-white films in general, and sad, mushy films in particular.

During an extended scene of pathos, April sniffed loudly and Jake passed her a box of tissues without taking his eyes off the flickering set. She scooted closer to him and his arm slipped around her shoulders. Soon they were cuddled together, her head resting on his chest.

Jake wasn't watching the movie; his apparent concentration was an act to cover his growing arousal. All he could think about was the exquisite weight of April's head where it pressed against his heart. Couldn't she hear its ragged pounding? He was achingly aware of the strawberry scent of her hair and the silky feel of it on his arm. Some of the tears she had shed over the movie had dripped onto his inner thigh and threatened to burn through the faded denim of his jeans.

He swallowed hard when her hand unwittingly rested on his leg, igniting inner fires that if left unchecked, could easily flare out of control. Didn't she know what she was doing to him? Had she no idea of how badly he wanted her? Of how much he needed more than her friendship? His hand covered hers and their fingers intertwined. He squeezed her shoulder and she slipped deeper into what was rapidly becoming an embrace.

Jake groaned and hoped it hadn't been audible. God, the woman was wearing him down, and if something didn't happen soon, he didn't hold out much hope for his sanity. No wonder he had never become so emotionally involved with a woman before—it was too damn much work. But April was worth it, he kept telling himself. She deserved more than one of his practiced seductions. In fact, he couldn't have pulled one off if he wanted to. She was different, and his tried-and-true techniques would seem a crude betrayal in the face of her trusting innocence.

He'd told her that he would take things easy, and while self-denial wasn't something that came readily to him, he vowed to keep that promise. One wrong move now could ruin everything.

"April?"

"Yes?" she answered absently, fully absorbed in the screen heroine's dilemma and oblivious to his.

"April, I have to go home," he said gruffly.

She looked up in surprise, the pupils of her wide blue eyes dilated and dreamy-looking. His gaze slid downward, and all he could see were the moist, delicate lips he had savored before. He knew exactly how they would feel beneath his touch: soft and warm and yielding. He knew they would open to him, inviting him to taste her sweetness. He knew that if he gave in to the impulse, it would be more than a kiss, it would be a sensual prelude.

Suddenly, reliving past kisses was not enough. He traced her lips with a fingertip and felt the heat building up inside him. She seemed to hold her breath as he stroked her cheek, and then she sighed as his hands wove slowly through her hair. His gaze held hers, and his lips were drawn inexorably to hers. The excruciating moment of anticipation seemed to last a lifetime.

April's resistance dissolved under Jake's heated onslaught, and she felt herself melting into his warmth. When she pressed her hand against his chest and felt the pounding of his heart, her own heartbeat picked up speed to match. The kiss lasted for a long time, and when he pulled away from her, she drew him back. Her tongue slipped into his mouth and she felt his hard body shudder, felt his arms tighten around her.

"My God, Red," he whispered, "you're killing me."

She smiled against his lips and teased, "But what a way to go."

His honorable intentions could be stretched only so far, and he eased her back onto the couch. "You're making my life a living hell, woman. I don't think I want to be your friend anymore," he pouted.

"Why not?"

He brushed the auburn veil of hair aside and dropped little kisses on her nose, chin, and forehead. "Because I want to be your lover."

"Are the two mutually exclusive?"

"I don't know. I've never had a friend for a lover or vice versa."

"I should think it could be a most rewarding state of affairs."

Jake groaned. The pain of wanting her was a physical ache. "Please, don't say 'affairs' unless you mean it."

She smiled and traced his lips as he had traced hers. "Sorry."

They heard the girls giggling and quickly resumed their former positions on the couch, with an entire seat cushion separating them. They trained their eyes on the television set in time to see the closing credits roll by.

"Okay, you two," Molly said in a stern voice. "What's going on in here?"

"Nothing," Jake and April answered in unison as they tried not to laugh.

"Nothing?" Molly turned to Staci. "Dark room, romantic movie, two lonely people, and nothing happened. We've got our work cut out for us, kid."

Two days later, April received official word from the bank. Her loan application had been rejected. It was anticlimactic and no big surprise. It wasn't as if her dream had died suddenly and without warning; it was more like its final life-support had been switched off.

When Jake called that night, he knew before he asked that things had gone badly. April's voice no longer held the cheerful optimism, the I'm-going-down-fighting determination, that he had come to expect. Her pain was his pain. And it was totally unnecessary. If she would only let him, he could make it go away with the wave of a pen.

"Look, I'll sign the loan with you." Before she could protest, he added, "This will be your baby, you'll be the boss. I'll be a silent partner, just a name on a piece of paper. What do you say?"

His voice was low and purposefully seductive, and April had to remind herself to resist him. For a moment she was nearly lulled into accepting his seemingly harmless offer, but every time she turned around, she ran headlong into the wall of pride she had erected. If she obligated herself to him in such a way, she'd lose what little power she had in the relationship. Even the nature of their association would change drastically.

Indebtedness would make saying "yes" to him in the future impossible, and anything more than business between them would be reduced to an exchange of favors. It all came down to the old adage about not mixing business with pleasure. Being both partners and lovers could complicate things in each relationship.

"Thanks, Jake, but no. It's time for Plan B." It could scarcely be called a plan, since the idea had only just occurred to her.

"Plan B?" he asked, his tone filled with suspicion.

"I still have a large sum of money in an account back in

Iowa. I set it aside from Caleb's insurance for Staci's future and for my old age, but maybe our present needs it more."

Jake's reaction was immediate. "You don't have to do that. Immodest as it sounds, with my name behind you, even the most conservative bank will lend you the money."

"Jake . . ." she warned.

"We need to discuss this in person. I'll be right over."

Before she could demur, the phone went dead and she imagined she heard his car's powerful engine revving in the distance. Without time to consider what she was going to say to him, he was on her doorstep.

"Listen," he said without preamble, filling her small living room with his overpowering presence. "This is no sudden impulse of mine. I've been thinking about doing something like this for a long time now." He pulled her down next to him on the sofa. "You know the problem with professional sports?"

April was amazed at how his nearness could set her senses whirling. Every time she saw him she was struck anew by how big and handsome he was. "Signal when you're changing subjects, will you? The problem with professional sports? Let me guess. Ego inflation among athletes?"

Jake grinned wryly. "Very funny. No, the problem with sports is that an athlete reaches his peak when he's still relatively young." He seemed to reconsider. "Maybe not in golf, but in just about everything else. Injuries or declining performance push him out of the game early, so what does he do then?"

April had no idea of where the conversation was leading. "Model pantyhose? Sell orange juice? Appear in bad movies?"

"Maybe. If a guy has a big enough name. But what about all the not-so-greats? The jocks who become local heroes but never achieve much national recognition?"

"I don't know, Jake," she said in exasperation. "Maybe they go into their father's wheel-balancing business."

"Exactly!" He smacked his fist down on the coffee table, then leaned back as though his point had been made.

Now she was really confused. "Are you saying that for a long time now you've had this burning desire to go into the wheel-balancing business?"

Jake rolled his eyes toward heaven. "Pay attention. What I'm trying to say is that a lot of ex-jocks go into businesses they don't really enjoy because they have no choice. I propose to give them a choice."

"And just how will you do that?"

"By searching out retiring sports stars and getting them started in the club or restaurant business in the area where they're best known. I can help set up the business end of things. Why let my MBA molder in a drawer? I might as well get some mileage out of it. They'll trade on their local celebrity, and with careful management, I should recoup my investment in a matter of a few years."

When he was finished, April said, "That's a great idea, Jake. I say go for it."

"What about you?" He leaned toward her and raised a questioning brow. "Are you going to 'go for it'?"

"Afraid not. Since I have no celebrity status to trade on, it wouldn't help either of us."

"I'll provide the name and the financing. You provide the creativity and muscle."

April laughed. "It sounds like you have all the answers, but it just won't work. You and I want different things."

He kissed her lightly on the lips, and her eyes closed against her will. "I don't think so, my dear. I think we want exactly the same thing. I also think you'll be sorry someday if you don't take me up on this offer now."

April opened her eyes when no more kisses were forthcoming. "Maybe I will. But how can we have a 'someday' if I don't have a 'now'?"

"What's that supposed to mean? Of course you have a 'now.'"

She could tell that his confusion was genuine, and she

attempted to explain her position again. "I don't want or need a nice strong man to come to my rescue, no matter how tempting said man might be. I've told you that getting this business going on my own is something I need to do, and I'd hoped you could understand that. You've never had to prove yourself, Jake, but try to accept that I do."

"Just who do you have to prove yourself to? Your in-laws?"

"To myself."

Jake knew that nothing he could say would change her mind, but he could be just as stubborn as she was. He didn't like the idea of using subterfuge; however, if the situation warranted, he wouldn't be above it. He pretended to give in. "Just promise me you won't use your nest egg. It isn't wise to gamble with your security."

"If you're so sure I'm going to fail, I have to wonder why you want to back me," she said stiffly. She'd thought Jake believed in her.

"It's nothing against you. But the restaurant business can eat you alive. There're a lot of factors contributing to an individual's success or failure that have nothing to do with knowledge, skill, or expertise."

April drew a deep breath. "I know that. And I'm trying not to let it discourage me too much."

"I still want that promise." It was only one of several he longed to extract from her. Why did she have to be so proud? Things would be much simpler if only she would let him help her. She was too hardheaded to admit that she loved him as much as he loved her. "Promise?"

"Okay. I promise I won't use my own money until I've exploited all other resources."

He sighed and resisted the temptation to remind her that the most compliant resource she would ever find was sitting right beside her—not only willing, but anxious to be exploited.

CHAPTER EIGHT

DURING THE NEXT two weeks, April made the rounds of every lender in Jacksonville. All of them, including the Small Business Administration, turned down her loan application. After hearing countless times that a) she didn't have the business acumen necessary, b) the city didn't really need another restaurant, and c) her proposition was entirely too risky, she was plagued by doubts. Maybe they were right and she was wrong. Maybe she had been too filled with enthusiasm to view the project objectively.

Well, she wasn't so filled with enthusiasm now. Her faith in herself had slipped a few notches, and she was afraid to risk the money she'd saved for the future. If it were just herself, she wouldn't hesitate, but there was Staci to consider. She simply could not gamble her daughter's education and security on a venture that according to the experts, was doomed from the beginning.

The names and faces of the loan officers she had talked to blurred in her mind, but she recalled one who was kind enough to preface his rejection with an explanation. "Mrs. Conway," he'd said, "it's not simply a financial decision we're dealing with here. Starting a business is an important lifestyle decision. Your restaurant might be the best in the world, your food the tastiest, your service the most impeccable. Even if you had all the money you needed, all the know-how and business savvy, it won't work unless you are willing to give it everything you've got. Those other things won't be enough."

When she protested, the man held up a hand. "Please, let me finish. You have a young daughter, and you strike me as the type of mother who is intensely involved with her child. Have you considered how much you'll have to give up in time and energy to get this business started?"

April sighed, no longer willing to be angered over what was certainly a form of discrimination, even if well-intentioned. "I've thought about the sacrifices involved. My daughter and I have discussed them, and I can cope with the responsibilities and the single-mindedness required to make the business go. But frankly, sir, I have to wonder if you would be as concerned about my personal life if I were a man." He had looked abashed at that and had quickly terminated the meeting.

Now, after so many discouraging words, April was ready to admit defeat. She met Jake at the beach, where he was on location for a tourism commercial. During a break, he told her not to give up.

"Come on, Red," he said. "Don't let those tight-fisted bankers have the last word. Take me on as a partner and we'll prove to them once and for all how far off the mark they are."

"And just how would we do that, Jake? Once you become involved, any success we achieve will be credited to you, not to me. I know that discrimination and prejudice against women are supposed to be dead issues, but believe me, they're alive and well in the business world. Even the female loan officers turned me down."

He reached over and lifted her chin. "Maybe you look so sweet and innocent that they're afraid you don't have the killer instinct necessary for survival."

"They won't take time to find out."

"Because they're fools, Red. I know you have that fighting spirit, but damned if I see any of it now."

"So much rejection has made me question myself. I may no longer be as sure that I can pull it off, but wanting the restaurant is not just a whim."

"Of course not. You've put a lot of thought and effort into this thing already."

"I've put more than that into it, Jake. I've put hope into it. This was going to be my chance to find out who I am and what I'm capable of. An opportunity to walk the tightrope of independence without a net. Always there's been someone there to catch me if I fell, and I've never risked a thing. This business was supposed to be my big solo number."

He saw the anguish in her eyes and was torn. He understood what she was saying, and yet he felt that she was being unnecessarily obtuse. How was he going to convince her that the restaurant had nothing to do with independence? That exalted state had to come from within.

"True independence can come only when you trust yourself. There's nothing wrong with accepting help from people who care about you," he suggested softly.

"I know," she said with a sad smile. "And the fact that you want to help me means a great deal. But I can see now that my mistake was in dreaming too big. I'm a country girl, and maybe I'd be better off with a little diner in Strawberry Point. You know, start small and work my way up."

Her words made Jake's heart tighten. "Don't talk like that. You're just feeling sorry for yourself right now because you've suffered a few setbacks."

She glared at him and he amended, "Okay. A lot of setbacks. Don't be such a pessimist. I have a feeling that things will start going your way soon." In fact, he was sure they would.

Jake walked with her down the beach while the director waited for the cloud cover to clear. The sun and sea, to say nothing of the stimulating company, should have taken her mind off her worries, but all April could think about was how she was going to tell Joe Castelli that she was withdrawing her offer.

When she went to pick up Staci, she found the two girls playing in the pool under Conchata's watchful eye. April had come to like the perky little woman who lovingly ran roughshod over Jake and Molly and who had extended her warmth to Staci.

Staci wanted to stop at the mall, and by the time April got home, it was past six. She procrastinated all evening, sitting by the phone trying to summon the nerve to call Joe and tell him the deal was off. When she did call early the next day, what he had to say both stunned and elated her.

"I've been thinking, Mrs. Conway." She had asked him to call her April, but he still used the formal address. "What's the point of dragging the banks in on this? You've got some good ideas, and I believe you're going to make it. I'll carry the note on the Onion and you can repay me out of the profits."

April could not respond immediately. She was too excited by the prospect of recapturing a dream she had felt slipping away from her. This was the turning point. This was the chance she had wanted.

"Mrs. Conway? You there?"

"Oh, yes, Joe, I'm here. I don't know what to say."

"Try 'yes' and let's hear how that sounds."

"Yes. Yes. Yes. Joe, you've made me a very happy woman."

"Heck, I haven't done a thing. I'm not a gambler, but I usually bet on a sure thing."

"I insist on giving you something up front. A down payment. How much would it take?"

"No need to do that," he demurred. "I don't owe any money on the place."

"I won't accept your offer unless you agree to some

earnest money. Say, ten thousand? So you can get that bait shop?"

"If you insist, ten thousand would be just fine."

And so the deal was concluded. Only the paperwork remained to be done. When she hung up the phone, April felt dizzy with excitement. This was too good to be true. The thought skittered briefly through her mind, but in her happiness, she didn't pause to consider the significance of it.

She called Jake and invited him to a picnic supper on the beach, her treat, but refused to tell him why she was celebrating. This kind of news was best delivered face-to-face and followed by a long congratulatory kiss. She knew that the work was just beginning, that getting the restaurant operational and running in the black would be a long upward climb, but just knowing she now had the chance to tackle the job gave her confidence.

The confidence gave her a new sense of power, and that gave her daring. Daring that made her regret the "friends-only" rule she had insisted apply to her relationship with Jake. He'd shown restraint she would have sworn he didn't possess, and the fact that he had respected her wishes only endeared him to her more. It also frightened her.

Someone with Jake the Rake's reputation would not stick around unless he genuinely cared for her. If all he was after was an affair, there were untold numbers of females willing to oblige him. Including herself. He was funny and charming and to-die-for handsome. He wasn't preoccupied with himself but was thoughtful to a fault. What woman in her right mind wouldn't want his attention?

What scared her was his seriousness. A wolf on the make she could handle, but every time she looked at Jake, she could see the longing in his eyes. A longing for commitment and permanency that she wasn't ready for. Yet. She hoped to someday remarry and be part of a family again, to give Staci a father and herself a lifelong partner. But she just wasn't ready to go back into marriage yet. It was too soon. She had been happily married for ten years and had enjoyed the security marriage offered. But right now, she wanted to learn to live with herself.

She couldn't expect Jake to wait for her. He'd never known the warmth of a loving, long-lasting relationship. He'd been so young when he'd taken on the responsibilities of fatherhood alone, and she knew he wanted and deserved to be part of a complete family circle. How inopportune that they had met at precisely this time in their lives, a time when they wanted such different things from life.

"All right," he said when she stopped her car on a deserted stretch of beach. "You've kept me in suspense long enough. You said you had some good news, but I want details, woman, details."

She tossed him a blanket and retrieved the picnic basket she had packed with an array of delicatessen goodies. "In time, my good man," she evaded. She handed him a bag containing a bottle of good champagne, two plastic wineglasses, and a corkscrew opener. "First things first."

They selected a spot and spread the blanket. Jake uncorked the bottle and the bubbly sprayed them both. Laughing, they filled their glasses and April held hers aloft. "A toast to Jacksonville's newest entrepreneur! Me."

"Red! You got the loan." He pulled her into his arms for the congratulatory kiss she had expected and champagne sloshed over the rims of their glasses.

"Not exactly. You'll never believe what happened."

He would, but he'd let her tell it anyway. "What?"

"When I called Joe and told him the deal was off, he offered to carry the note. I don't know how he can afford to be so generous, but at this point, I'm not asking questions."

"That's great, honey. I'm really happy for you." Jake tried to force some enthusiasm into his voice.

She pulled back and stared hard at him. "That's funny. You don't sound very happy. Didn't you want me to get the restaurant?"

"More than anything else in the world. I'm just speechless." The less he said, the better off he'd be. That way he wouldn't betray himself.

"Maybe I should alert the media," she joked. "Jake the Rake, speechless at last." She opened the hamper and handed him a corned-beef sandwich and a dill pickle.

"I still want the details. Tell me all about it."

Between bites, she obliged and became so carried away that she also told him all about how she was planning to do some of the remodeling herself in an effort to save money and to keep her nest egg intact.

"Do you know anything about that sort of thing?" he asked skeptically.

"I helped Caleb paint the dairy barn bright red once, and I've hung enough wallpaper to do the White House. Back in Strawberry Point, I frequently bartered my paperhanging expertise. I did a whole house for Mrs. Cluny, the piano teacher, in exchange for Staci's lessons, a kitchen for the dressmaker for a new fall suit, and the front room of Aaron's Shoe Salon for winter boots for Staci and myself."

"Sounds like you know your wallpaper," Jake teased.

"You'd better believe it. It's a gift I have. I'm also pretty handy with a hammer and nails."

Jake was delighted by her happy, carefree attitude. No matter what happened, seeing her eyes glow like this was worth it. "My, my. Do you have any other hidden talents I should know about?" He recklessly tossed the remnants of his sandwich over his shoulder and crawled toward her across the blanket, the look of the devil on his handsome features.

April had to speak up to be heard over the squawking gull that swooped down to take advantage of the unexpected buffet. "So many it boggles the mind." She pretended alarm. "Jake! What are you doing?"

With both hands on her shoulders, he eased her back on the blanket and positioned himself above her. They had watched the sunset but there was still enough light left for her to see the gleam in his eye.

"You mean you don't know?" he asked so seriously that she had to laugh. "I'll explain. First I'm going to push your sweater aside so I can smother your shoulder with tickly kisses." He demonstrated what he had in mind. "While you're gasping with pleasure, my other hand will slip underneath to cup your breast and tease your little pink nipple to attention."

"God, Jake!" April tried not to writhe beneath him, but the sensual combination of words and actions was enough to make her forget about their differences.

He was far from finished. "Since I'm an equal-opportunity lover, I'm going to give your other breast equal time while I nibble your neck and whisper loving words in your ear." He did just that, and she felt her resistance drain away like honey from an overturned jar.

"Jake . . ." She was going to tell him they should stop while they still could, but his lips silenced her. After a hungry kiss that shattered the last of her resolve and left her quivering expectantly beneath him, he picked up his play-by-play description.

"Now Keegan demonstrates his full-court skills and the fans go wild," he murmured as his hand trailed downward from her breast. His lips followed suit, and he kissed her all the way down to her bare toes and back up to her neck.

She gasped when his hand slipped beneath the elastic waistband of her shorts and into the filmy confines of her panties. His lips reclaimed hers, and she returned his kisses with reckless abandon, giving herself up completely to the passion of his slow, sensuous massage.

His gentle touch was coaxing, yet it demanded that she reach for and attain fulfillment. She felt the heat radiating outward until she feared it would consume her. She arched against him, moaning his name as waves of rapture washed over her. She lay back, sated, but he wasn't through with her yet. His thrusting tongue ravished her mouth as his expert touch sent her to even higher levels of ecstasy. Just when she thought she would die from pleasure, he lay down beside her and cradled her in his arms. He covered her face with hot kisses and murmured, "Tell me what you want, Red."

"I want you to love me."

"I do."

"I want it all." She had been unbuttoning his shirt as they talked, and now she pushed it away. His skin was hot, and her hands felt the play of muscles on his chest. "Show me, Jake."

"I thought you'd never ask."

He expelled a long sigh and deftly removed the rest of her clothing, kissing and caressing the skin he revealed. His heated anticipation escalated when she removed his pants, and the fire raced through him as he brought his stomach against hers. His body burned, sought—and so did hers—through moments of impossibly sweet, unbearably wonderful straining.

The ferocity of his passion created a wild ecstasy of her senses. She was lost in the hunger of his exploring hands, and clung to him. His forceful vitality raced through her. She reached for the ultimate pleasure and answered his urging with her own whispered words of joy.

Jake heard her and exulted in her pleasure as he found a sudden, cascading release. Never had he felt so moved by an act of lovemaking, but then love had never been a part of it before. He was glad they'd waited, glad they had taken time for soft romance. April was the answer to all of his hopes, to all of his longings. The difference she had made in his life was incalculable, and he hoped he had touched a wellspring within her as she had within him.

April was weak and confused, drowned in a flood tide of emotions, yet exhilarated by the liberation of her mind and body. Loving Jake was an experience unlike any she had ever known, and she cursed herself for denying her

Out of the Blue

feelings for him for so long. There could be no more denying. "Jake?"

He held her fiercely, protectively, as though he would never let her go. "Yes, love?"

"I think there's something you should know."

"What's that, Red?"

"I love you."

"Good." He brushed the tendrils away from her face and held her tenderly. There could be no more talking; he wanted to concentrate on the woman in his arms, on his love for her. "We're going to be very happy someday."

While the needs of their bodies could no longer be denied, it was still too early for him to say the words he longed to say: that she would be his forever. He had always had the gift of gab, been full of blarney as Chaz had often remarked, and he had talked himself into and out of many a sticky situation. But this was different. He couldn't tell her how much he cared, how much he wanted and needed her, because it was too soon and she wouldn't believe him.

She had said she loved him and that was enough. For now.

They lay in silence on the blanket in the sand for a long time, watching the stars wink overhead and listening to the steady, rhythmic pounding of the surf. Both were trying to reconcile themselves to the surprising depth of their feelings, to adjust to this newest development.

The ride home was quiet, and when April parked in front of his house, he held her face in his big hands and dropped a brief kiss on her nose.

"Still friends?" he asked.

"Best friends," she confirmed.

Once the loan papers were signed, plans proceeded rapidly. The Big Onion was closed for the first time in fifteen years, its former owner happily retired from the restaurant business and ensconced in the bait-and-tackle shop of his dreams. A sign on the door proclaimed that the establishment would reopen soon under new management.

The new owner worked hard every day to make that claim a reality. April hired a contractor friend of Joe's to do the heavy remodeling and build the alfresco area but insisted on doing much of the decorating herself, explaining that the more she did, the more money she would save. Jake recruited off-season Jags to construct area dividers and paint walls for wages of beer, food, and friendly camaraderie, and they were only too happy to help out their favorite teammate and his woman.

So that she could reach her self-imposed grand-opening date, Jake and April worked side by side, often until late at night, drinking wine and stripping greasy wallpaper. They talked about many things when they were alone: their childhoods, their parents, their daughters. April told Jake about her marriage, and Jake told her about Shelley. They shared their views on politics, the economy, criminal justice, and nuclear warfare. Between busy schedules and inquisitive children, their moments of stolen pleasure were regrettably few. However, what they lacked in frequency was compensated for in intensity.

April was so absorbed by her new business venture that she didn't have much time to think about the future of their relationship. Jake, on the other hand, had plenty of time, but he chose not to make waves. For now it was enough just to be near her. He was getting to know her better, and the more he learned about her, the more he loved her.

Their combined efforts were paying off, and April was thrilled by the progress they were making. Once the dark booths lining the walls were removed, the dining room opened up to exciting new possibilities. The top third of the ten-foot-high walls were painted pale mauve, and a trellis type of wallpaper with a subtle pattern of twining green ivy and mauve blossoms covered the lower two thirds, the division marked by a kelly-green wooden molding. The vaulted ceiling was painted white, and oak fans were installed to boost the air conditioner's cooling capacity.

New beveled stained-glass replaced the grimy glass in the front window, and new mirrors were installed behind the bar, which had been stripped of its dark stain to reveal the light oak wood beneath. Oversized squares of black-and-white floor tiles added to the room's completely new look.

April's oak tables and chairs had been delivered the day before, and the mauve-and-green tablecloths and napkins were stacked on the fully equipped bar. The kitchen had been remodeled and furnished with gleaming new appliances and shining pots and pans. Tableware, stainless-steel utensils, and glassware were washed and stored on the refurbished shelves.

"I like it," Jake mused as he surveyed the room from several different perspectives. He had a hammer in his hand and a carpenter's apron full of nails tied around his narrow waist.

"It doesn't look much like the old Onion, does it?" asked Chaz from his perch atop a tall ladder. He and Jake had been hanging shelves high on the walls to hold plants in brass pots and the collection of bric-a-brac April had amassed.

Looking for art-deco period pieces as well as nostalgia items, she had dragged Jake and the girls on many a weekend treasure-hunting expedition. Jake claimed that he was allergic to the second-hand dust found in antique shops and flea markets, but he had accompanied her because he couldn't bear to let her go alone.

"It doesn't look a thing like the old Onion. What I want to know," Jake paused and stared pointedly at April, "is what it does look like. You have to give this place a name, Red."

"Yeah," chimed in Molly. "We can't just keep calling it 'the place' the way people call their kid 'the baby' until it goes to school."

"I know," she admitted. Jake and the girls had been after her for weeks to choose a name, but so far she hadn't come up with anything she liked. "I'll pick something soon."

Jake climbed the other ladder to help Chaz, muttering in a Stan Laurel voice, "I certainly hope so, Ollie."

That night, after Conchata had taken Molly and Staci to a concert, Jake turned out the lights in the restaurant and talked April into a rest period, complete with passionate kisses that led to a wonderfully unique experience. Afterward, he retrieved a bottle of wine from the refrigerator and poured each of them a glass. He had been wanting to discuss something with her for a while now, but hadn't had the opportunity. Taking her hand, he led her to one of the small tables in the back, where they sat down.

"You've made it clear, Red, that you don't want or need me as a business partner," he began soberly. "Would you consider hiring me as a host? I could help bring in the local sports trade. Jacksonville folks are serious about basketball, and immodest as it sounds, I am basketball in this town. At least I was."

April sipped her wine. "I couldn't afford you. I've heard about those six-figure contracts of yours."

"They're for superstar athletes. Broken-down has-beens work cheap."

"Broken-down has-been?" She looked him up and down meaningfully. "I'm glad I didn't meet you when you were in your prime. I never would have survived the experience."

He laughed, leaned over and stole a kiss. "Look, I need the job," he pleaded with mock resignation. "I'll bus tables, wash dishes, whatever. I like this place, and I want to be close to my favorite entrepreneur."

Not only that, but for the first time, he had done something that his conscience wouldn't leave alone. This little ice-breaking talk might make a full confession easier.

April got up and stood behind his chair, wrapping her

arms around his neck. She had come to care so much for him that she couldn't bear the idea of opening the restaurant without him. She still didn't understand exactly what they had together, but she had chosen to follow Suze's advice and not look a gift horse in the mouth. She never had fit the contemporary image of chic or glamorous. She had been described by many as sweet and unpretentious, but if asked to give a one-word description of her appearance, she was wont to say "wholesome." She had "Mom" written all over her, that middle-America, apple-pie look that eliminated her as a candidate for most men's erotic fantasies. She was just happy that it hadn't eliminated her from Jake's.

She didn't feel sweet and wholesome around him. His blatant masculinity made her acutely aware of her own gender. His simmering glances and feverish kisses filled her with images of delightful possibilities and ignited a few fantasies of her own. There was no doubt about it, with Jake she felt sexy. He made her think about things she hadn't thought about for a long time.

"So?" he asked. "Am I in, or am I doomed to stand in unemployment lines forever?"

"What are you talking about?"

"Retirement. I've decided to end my basketball career on a high note. I won't be going back when the new season starts, so I'll need something to keep me busy and out of trouble."

April couldn't imagine working all those long, necessary hours without his twinkling eyes and irreverent comments to lighten the load. She would agree to almost anything just to have an excuse to spend more time with him.

"You have a deal, friend. The place wouldn't be the same without you. What's it going to cost me?"

He pulled her onto his lap and kissed her, deep and hard. "It'll cost you plenty, but money need never change hands." He dipped her backward, smooched her neck, and lifted up the front of her T-shirt to peek inside. "Yep, it'll cost you plenty, lady," he said with a lascivious leer.

April scrambled to her feet. "Really, sir. Is that any way to conduct employee relations?"

"Employee relations, huh?" He appeared to consider. "You know," he said as though making a wondrous discovery, "that's my second-favorite type of relations."

CHAPTER NINE

GETTING READY FOR the grand opening consumed all of April's time. She hired an experienced cook who tried her recipes out on Jake and the guys and a menu was gradually formulated. She placed orders with vendors for food and liquor, and once all the inspections were passed, she acquired the appropriate licenses.

Molly and Staci helped select items for the children's menu and suggested giving the kids coloring sheets and crayons to keep them busy while they waited for their food. April thought it a great idea. She recruited the girls to water the plants and taught them how to fold napkins that would stand up in little cone shapes.

Joe dropped in regularly to inspect their progress and to boast about the life of Riley he was living out in Jacksonville Beach.

"You know, Joe," April told him one day, "if you ever want to get back in the rat race, I could use a good bartender."

"Nah. I'm glad I'm out of it. The rats were winning."

"If you change your mind, let me know."

He looked thoughtful, and April suspected that he was a bit bored with selling bait. He had been in harness for too many years to suddenly be turned out to pasture. "Maybe after the tourist season, I could put in an evening or two."

She acted busy to hide her amusement. "Just say the word."

Later, after everyone else had left, she sat doodling at a table, having just compiled a wine list to send to the printer the next day. Jake placed a cup of coffee beside her pad and sat down across from her.

"I hope all that concentration is directed toward selecting a name for this place," he said with an air of someone who didn't think there was a chance in the world it might be.

"You sound like a broken record, Jake." She put her pencil aside and grinned at him.

"You do realize that we'll be opening in less than two weeks?"

She liked the comforting sound of that "we." "Thirteen days, to be exact."

"Precisely my point. You've performed miracles in getting things ready, but there's still a lot left to do."

"I was just thinking the same thing," she concurred.

"So what are we going to call this joint?"

"Please, sir," she said with mock indignation. "You may call it a restaurant, a bistro, a café, a watering hole, or a chic new in-place, but don't refer to it as a joint."

"I stand corrected. So what are we going to call all of the above?"

She laughed at his frustration. "I'm working on it."

"We still have to order the signs and get advance publicity out. The printer is waiting for a name to stamp on the menu covers and to print on the stationery you ordered."

"I know."

Jake's eyes narrowed. "Maybe what you need is an ultimatum. I have to go to Miami for a couple of days and I want you to promise you'll have a name picked out when I get back."

"Did the endorsement deal come through?" April knew

that he had been waiting for the results of negotiations with a prominent sports-shoe company. If the outfit met his price and standards, he would sign on as spokesman for its new line of court shoes.

"I got the word this afternoon, and they've already called a press conference to kick off the ad campaign."

April was glad it had worked out. She worried about his working in the restaurant for the mediocre wage she could afford to pay him. He'd need another source of income in order to maintain his present lifestyle. Of course she had no idea of what his net worth was; the only finances they had ever discussed were hers, but she was certain that with his business acumen, he would have made profitable investments.

"That's great. Did you get the money you wanted?"

Vague as ever, he answered, "Enough to keep Molly in U2 albums for a while."

She smiled and rubbed her temples, where a fatigue headache was pulsing. She had been in the restaurant since early morning and it was now nearly seven o'clock. Staci and Molly were over in a corner watching the portable television set Jake had provided, and she felt guilty that she'd spent so little time with her daughter lately. They'd lived on take-out food and experimental dishes the cook created. They went to bed late and arose early. The restaurant was eating up every minute of her time and all of her attention, and it wasn't even open yet.

She told herself that things would be different when the operation got rolling, when there was enough money to hire additional employees, including someone to relieve her in the evenings so she could spend more time at home with Staci. They had both known that it would be like this at first, as all-consuming as any other infant enterprise, and April was secure in the knowledge that their mother-daughter relationship was strong enough to survive it. But she still had a guilty feeling and rubbed her temples again in an unconscious gesture of stress.

Jake noticed her anguish and urged her to call it a night. "You've been working too hard. Why don't you go home and get some sleep? The way you're going, you'll be worn out before the opening."

"I have just a few more things to do, but you can go ahead. I appreciate all the help you've given me, and I know you miss Molly. Go home and spend some time with her before you leave for Miami."

"I think I'll take you up on that. But I want two promises from you before I go."

She looked at him in consternation. "Now it's two? I thought there was only one."

"Promise you'll select a name for this place before I get back, and promise me you'll go home soon."

"An easy yes to both. Once you and Molly leave, Staci will remember how tired and hungry she is and I'll have no choice."

"Smart kid." He called Molly and kissed April, who locked the front door behind them.

"Will you make me a hamburger for dinner?" Staci asked.

"Sure, honey, but wouldn't you rather stop at MacDonald's?"

Staci turned up her freckled nose. "Thanks for the offer, Mom, but we had breakfast and lunch there. Remember?"

April was stuffing papers into her briefcase. "So we did, baby. I forgot," she said absently as an unexpected idea began to form in her mind. She slipped back into the chair and dug her mechanical pencil out of her bag.

"Mom-om-om! I thought we were going."

"We are. Just a minute." She turned to a fresh page in her pad and began to sketch.

Staci sighed and sank down in the chair Jake had vacated. "Will this be a sixty-second minute or an hour-and-a-half minute?"

"Um-hum," was all April said.

A few minutes ago when Jake left, she had seen him

framed in the doorway, the last rays of sunset glowing through the stained glass and illuminating him in brilliant refracted color. When he turned and kissed her, he had seemed indistinguishable from the restaurant's facade, as much a part of it as the woodwork and glass. That was when the inspiration had come.

Or maybe it wasn't an inspiration at all. It was the sudden acknowledgment of something she had known for a long time. It was the overwhelming certainty that the best name for the restaurant she'd worked so hard for was JAKE'S. He was in it and of it, the reason she had struggled on in the face of enormous odds.

When she had come to Jacksonville, all she'd had was an idea, a concept. Through Jake that idea had become focused into an attainable reality. He had given her the courage to keep on trying, and he had taught her to laugh in the face of defeat. His continued efforts to convince her to let him underwrite the venture had made her even more determined to succeed on her own. Had he known that would happen? Had he used the reverse psychology that he must have suspected would work with her?

Through his outspoken, brash, "let-me-do-it-for-you" attitude, he had quietly urged her on. He had shored up her confidence and fueled her independence by offering her the free ride he knew she would reject. Yes, he had known what he was doing, she thought wryly. He understood her well.

Jake. Knowing him was a gift, his friendship a treasure. Loving him was a joy unlike any she had ever known before.

JAKE'S. The tempered masculine edge of the name contrasted in surprising and delightful ways with the ambience she had created in the restaurant. The name wasn't pretentious or self-conscious as were some of the others she had considered: THE GARDEN, TRUFFLES, CON BRIO. Jake's carried with it the same casual joie de vivre and warmth as the man, the same justified confidence and insouciance. The same attraction. She knew that, initially, people would come to the restaurant out of loyalty to its namesake, but it would be up to her to ensure their repeat business. In that way, they could work together, and be real partners.

It was perfect, and April's first impulse was to call Jake right away and advise him of her decision. But no, she thought as she put the finishing touches on her drawing, not yet. First she wanted to try the idea on for size, to let it settle into her consciousness.

But most of all, she wanted to think about what it meant. Not just professionally, but personally. Calling the place JAKE'S was definitely a commitment. It meant that she wanted him not only in her business, but in her life as well, and on a permanent basis. Because it ran counter to everything she'd told herself she wanted, she would have to understand that concept thoroughly before she could share it with him.

"Whatcha got there, Mom?" Staci turned the pad around for a better view of April's design for an elaborate neon sign. The work JAKE'S was written in flowing script, the letters surrounded by a twining border of leaves and stylistic blooms. Her eyes widened. "What does this mean?"

April smiled at her daughter, so filled with a rush of secret feelings that she wasn't sure she could answer. JAKE'S. JAKE'S place. JAKE'S woman. JAKE'S wife? She was astounded by the natural progression, as well as by how easily she accepted the idea.

"Mom? Are you really going to call it JAKE'S?"

"If you agree. What do you say?"

Staci's smile lit up her whole face. "I say yes. Molly will be so surprised."

April took the pad back. "You can't tell Molly yet, baby."

"Why not?"

"Because I want to tell Jake first. He's leaving in the morning for Miami, and I'll tell him as soon as he gets back. Can you keep a secret that long?"

Staci grimaced. "Do I have to?"

"For me? Please?"

Staci came around the table and sat on her mother's lap. She wrapped her arms around her neck and kissed her cheek. "For you, Mom, anything. But how long will Jake be gone?"

April laughed and shifted her daughter's weight. "A couple of days is all. In the meantime, we have a lot of work to do. I have to take this design to the sign company and order the printing."

"Alert the media?" Staci teased.

"Exactly. Like I said, we have a lot to do."

"Mom?"

"Yes, dear?"

"Can we at least eat first?"

The day before Jake was scheduled to return, Joe Castelli dropped by the restaurant, where April was going over the new set of account books she had just purchased. He presented her with a well-wrapped jack fish which she stored in the freezer, promising to invite him to dinner when things settled down and she had time to cook it. Then he inquired after Jake and the girls, who were spending the day at the beach with Conchata.

"Everyone's fine, Joe," April told him with a cheerful smile. She hadn't stopped smiling since she'd made her decision about Jake. Waiting for him to return was growing more difficult by the minute. "Things couldn't be better. The date for the opening is firm. In fact, I just talked to the newspaper about advertising. You'll be there won't you?"

"Darn tootin'. Wouldn't miss it. I want to be here to congratulate two of my favorite people on their new venture. It'll do my heart good to see you two working side by side." The older man looked around the room where he'd spent so many years, his hard, observant eyes taking in all the changes. "I like what you've done to the place, April." He looked at her anxiously. "Is it okay if I call you April?"

She tried not to grin. She had been urging him to do just that since the day they met. "Certainly, Joe."

"Good. Yeah, you got good taste. Maybe that's why you and Jake get along so well."

"How's that?"

"Jake's got good taste, too. He picked you, didn't he?"

"Joe, are you trying to flatter me? Because if you are, it's working."

"Nah. But you'll know what you want, and you're smart. I knew that the minute you started asking me questions about the Onion. Jake's smart, too. Smart enough to see through your cute outside to the brains and guts inside."

His appraisal didn't conjure up a very attractive picture; it was vivid, but April knew that Joe's heart was in the right place. "Thanks," she said with a laugh, "for what I'm pretty sure was a compliment."

Joe looked flustered, his heavy gray brows drawing together into a solid bushy line. "'Course it was a compliment. You're just the kind of woman Jake needs. Not one of them vacuum-headed tootsies I've seen him with. Most of those girls don't even bother to get to know the real Jake."

"The real Jake is a bit elusive."

"Maybe, but he's there. You just have to be willing to look. You know, I first met Jake when he was a rookie with the Jags. Twenty-two years old, fresh out of college. Did you know he went back in the off-season to earn his what-do-you-call-it?"

"MBA?" she supplied.

"Right. Took him a while, but he did it. And that little gal of his was just a mite then. His sister helped him out, but Jake was always there for that kid. Lots of nights the guys and their girl friends would be sitting around in here after a home game, eating burgers and drinking beer and having a good time, and I'd ask where Jake was. Know what they said?"

April shook her head, fascinated by this glimpse into Jake's past.

"They'd say, 'Oh, he had to get on home 'cause his baby's sick,' or some such as that. One time I remember they said Molly was waiting up for him and he went home to read her a story before she went to bed. Can you feature that?" Joe shook his head as if a highly paid young athlete who actually took care of his own child was a candidate for Ripley's *Believe It or Not*.

"He is her father, after all," April felt obliged to remind him.

"Yeah, but how many in his place would have done the same? Why, from the very first pro game he played, Jake had women fans screaming his name and sailing paper airplanes with their phone numbers onto the court. He was a damned good player and always received his share of publicity and attention. He was everybody's hero; men loved him because he played ball like a tiger, and women loved him because they thought he made love the same way." Joe looked away as if that comment embarrassed him. "That kind of thing might have turned the head of a lesser man. A lesser man would have been only too happy to foist his responsibilities off on someone else. But not Jake."

"No, not Jake."

"He's got something special, that boy. He has the ability to see through every kind of phoniness. He knows what he is and he's satisfied with himself. He's untouched, that's what he is," Joe pronounced proudly.

She wouldn't go that far, April mused. When he got back from Miami, Jake was going to be touched plenty. She concealed that thought with a nervous cough. "You're right, Joe. Jake is special. That's why I've decided to call this place JAKE'S. I want the restaurant to be special, too."

Joe reached over and patted her hand. "I'm pleased to hear you say that, April. Is there any chance things might . . . you know . . . work out between you two?"

"My father used to say, 'Even a blind pig finds an acorn once in a while.' I've been pretty blind, but luck was on my side. Jake hung in there until I came around."

"Told you he was smart. But frankly, when he came up with the idea of financing this place for you, I thought he was going to botch things up good. You struck me as the independent type, and I tried to tell him it wasn't fair to go behind your back. But you know Jake, he's not one to let go once he gets an idea." Joe's words trailed off when he saw the stricken look on April's face. "Whatsa matter, honey? Did I say something wrong?"

His words stunned April, and his voice sounded diluted and remote, as though it were coming to her from far away. What had he said about Jake going behind her back? She tried to untangle her thoughts long enough to respond. "Sorry, Joe. I guess I wasn't paying attention. What did you say?" Please, she implored silently, don't let it be true. Don't tell me that Jake put up the money for the restaurant.

Joe's sunbaked features furrowed with worry. "Am I talking out of school? I assumed Jake had told you about paying me off and carrying the note himself." She blanched and he added, "He didn't tell you, did he?"

She tried to compose herself, but the news of Jake's deception burned through her like a summer fire. "Maybe *you* should tell me, Joe," she said quietly.

He shook his head. "Nah, this is between you and Jake. I've said way too much already. Damn," he muttered under his breath. "Leave it to me to blunder around and put my big foot in it."

"Joe, I think I deserve to hear this. Clearly, Jake had no intention of telling me, so it's only right that you do." Jake, how could you do this? April's tears were not visible, but she was sobbing on the inside.

"Well-l-l."

"Please."

"Okay. Jake came to see me here at the restaurant. He'd

been out to the beach shooting some kind of commercial, and he told me you'd driven out to talk."

"I remember," she said. "That was the day I became officially rejected by every bank in Jacksonville, as well as by some out-of-town banks. I did go out to the beach that day, and I did tell Jake I was calling it quits."

"That's right. He told me you were giving up and thinking about going back to Iowa. Said he couldn't let that happen."

"Did he say why?"

Joe looked at her with surprise. "He sure did." He clearly disliked discussing the matter, and his next words were underlined with embarrassment. "He said that he loved you too much to see you hurt and that if you went home, he'd never have a chance to prove it."

"He chose a most unfortunate way to do so." The first shock was over and April's heart was steeled with anger. "He knew how much I wanted to do this on my own. To think he tricked me, deceived me."

"No, honey, it wasn't like that," Joe protested. "Jake, he had a hard time making the decision. He knew what he was doing and what he might be risking. Hell, he sat there at that bar and drank and worried and worried and drank. Never saw him resort to alcohol before. Anyhow, he finally said, 'If April loses this place, I'll lose her,' and that was the way it ended."

"How much did he give you?"

"Now don't look at me like you just found out we conspired to overthrow the government or something."

"I'm sorry, Joe. I'm not angry with you. But I need to know the exact size of my debt to Mr. Keegan."

"Mr. Keegan?" Joe didn't attempt to hide his dismay. "Just like that he goes from being Things-Couldn't-Be-Better-Jake to How-Much-Do-I-Owe-Mr. Keegan?"

"How much, Joe?"

"I don't want to do this."

"How much, Joe?"

"He offered me ninety-two five, but when you insisted on giving me ten, he paid me the difference." It came out in a rush, as though he were relieved to have it out in the open after all.

"Ninety-two thousand five hundred? But the note I signed was for only forty-seven five less the ten thousand down payment."

"Yeah." Joe grimaced. "See, Jake, he figured he could afford it more than you."

"Did he?" She was angry, but there was more to it than that. Never had April felt such bitter disappointment. Never had she so misjudged someone, and never had she been made to look like such a fool. She had never thought to love again, but she had. Oh, how she loved him. It was a painful realization, but it seemed that Jake Keegan wasn't worthy of that love at all. He'd seemed so sincere, so thoughtful, so understanding of her needs. He'd fooled her. In reality, he was what she had thought him at their first meeting: a charming manipulator, who thought first and foremost of himself.

Joe patted her hand in a comforting gesture. "Don't think bad of the boy, and don't be too hard on him, April. He did what he thought he had to do, and he really did suffer making that decision."

"Too bad. After all that, he still made the wrong one."

The hurt propelled April home, and she considered calling Jake in Miami. If she talked to him now, while she was still in a state of shock, maybe she wouldn't say things she didn't mean. Maybe she could focus on her own feelings and not get too tied up in his motives. Motives that wouldn't stand close scrutiny. She was sure that Jake had not been completely honest with Joe. What he had done wasn't born of love, it was conceived in deceit.

She decided to confront him in person. She would be in better control if she sorted her feelings out in advance, if she had her anger to sustain her through what was sure to be a crushing showdown. But even that was delayed because he called that night to tell her he loved her and would be tied up in Miami for a few more days. She tried to sound normal on the phone, but it was an extremely tense conversation and when she hung up, she shed a few tears.

Now, in an effort to keep busy, she was working alone in the restaurant. Earlier in the day, she had picked up the cream-colored stationery from the printer. He had promised her a rush job, and he had come through. So far, she had been unable to open any of the boxes and had almost burst into tears when the man had shown her a sample sheet for her approval. The only mistake was that in the left-hand corner her name was listed as proprietor. That would have to be changed.

Concentrating on her accounts, she was startled when she heard a light tap on the front door. Glancing up, she saw Jake standing outside, looking gorgeously rumpled from his flight. What was he doing here? She stayed where she was, unable to move toward the door.

He tapped again and gave her a silly yoo-hoo wave. "Red? Come on, let me in." His words were muffled by the glass door.

She unlocked it and he stepped inside. Before he could speak, she said, "I wasn't expecting you."

Jake was about to sweep her into his arms, but her accusing tone stilled the action. He gripped her shoulders and looked down into her face in an effort to discover what was wrong. "I'm early." He inclined his head for the welcoming kiss he had been anticipating ever since he left, but she wrenched out of his grasp and turned away.

"Yes, you are."

"After our conversation last night—if you want to call me talking and you listening in stony silence at the other end a conversation—I had the feeling I should get back here as soon as possible. Something's wrong, Red. What is it?"

April wasn't ready for this. The anger was there, but the

hurt was just as strong. Unable to hold it inside any longer, she blurted, "I know, Jake."

He had speculated during the trip home on just what could have happened to take the warmth and happiness out of her voice. She had been terse on the phone, her words hollow, as though something terrible had happened.

But now that he was here, he could see that it was no family problem, no crisis in Iowa. Something had to be seriously wrong between them for her to avert her face from his kiss. She backed up a few steps and waited silently. Her aggressive stance, with her arms folded across her breasts and her chin held high, was an eloquent expression of body language.

"Are you going to explain that remark," he asked, "or wait patiently while I figure it out?"

April's world was about to come apart and there was nothing she could do about it. She wanted to rush at him, to pound his chest with her fists, to curse him, and to weep like a character caught up in the anguish of a Greek tragedy. But she did none of those things. He had made a fool of her, but she still had her pride, and pride would see her through this. He never had to know how deeply his deception had hurt her.

"Why did you do it, Jake?" she asked in a voice that belied her inner turmoil. "Did you think you had to buy me?"

So, she'd found out about the financial arrangements. Damn, he should have told her about that long before now. He had tried to. Several times. But somehow he had always buried his head and pretended that if he didn't think about it, she wouldn't find out.

"It wasn't like that, April." He made a move toward her and she put a table between them.

"Tell me what it was like. And don't worry about explaining the 'how' of it. That I already know. What I want are the 'whys.'" Her voice was cold, distant, objective, as if she were no longer personally involved.

"I just couldn't bear to see you so disappointed. When you started talking about going back to Iowa, I was scared I'd lose you. I had it within my power to help you, to give us more time, to ensure a future for us, so I did. What is the crime in that?"

"The crime was in the betrayal. I thought I knew you, I thought you knew me. I thought you understood how important this was to me. But I was wrong. You didn't even think of me, you were thinking only of yourself. By going behind my back on this, you proved that you have no regard at all for my feelings."

"That isn't true." Jake knew he had made a mistake and that April's anger was totally justified. But he wouldn't let her think he didn't care. "I love you! I want you to marry me. I know what I did was wrong, and I apologize. Can't you forgive me?"

She shook her head. She was no longer sure he knew what love was; she had to discount his claim. Marriage? Unthinkable. "What you did is unforgivable."

"That's a bit strong, isn't it? Maybe my actions were misguided..."

Her laugh was hard, not really a laugh at all. "Misguided? That's a euphemistic way of phrasing it."

"If you hadn't been so damned stubborn and shortsighted—"

"Shortsighted! How dare you call me shortsighted! All I've been thinking about lately is the future."

"Will you kindly shut up and let me finish a sentence?" Jake's frustration grew by the minute, and he raked a hand through his hair. "I planned to tell you the truth."

"But you didn't."

"No, damn it, I didn't. I wanted to, but the time never seemed right. You were so caught up in your plans for the place, so preoccupied, that the subject just didn't come up."

"Did it ever occur to you to *bring* it up?" she asked icily.

"Yeah, frequently. I considered presenting you with the paid-off mortgage on opening night—the same night I planned to ask you to marry me, by the way."

"Don't do it, Jake," she warned. "That subject is closed."

Her words made something wither inside him. "I decided that sounded too premeditated, so I thought I might take a more casual approach: 'Pass the paint, and oh yes, I financed the joint for you.' Sorry," he apologized with a grin. "I forgot. You asked me not to call it a joint, didn't you?" He couldn't believe things were as bad as she was making them out to be, and his teasing tone was meant to josh her out of her black mood.

It didn't work. "You can call your place anything you want to," she said stonily.

"My place?"

"Your place." She strode to the bar, picked up one of the dark-green leather menu covers and thrust it into his hands.

He turned it over and saw the name JAKE'S stamped in gold in the center. "What's this?"

"While you were gone, I fulfilled my promise. I named the joint." She flung another piece of paper at him, which he could see was a drawing for a neon sign spelling out the same name. Slapping the key to the front door down on a nearby table, she said bitterly, "A fortunate choice, wouldn't you say?"

She'd named the place after him? Jake was still trying to comprehend the implications of that decision. Was he reading too much into it, or did it symbolize her willingness to let him into her life? Had she been on the verge of an emotional breakthrough when she found out what he had done? Damn!

"April, I don't want that key."

"Why not? After all, it belongs to you. The whole place is yours—lock, stock, and sauté pans."

"What about all the work you've put in? What about

your ten thousand dollars and everything you've spent on improvements?"

"Forget it. I plan to write that off as a bad investment."

"What about me?"

She raised a brow. "Like I said—"

"Look," he interrupted. "Let's don't get carried away here. Nothing that terrible has really happened. This is still your restaurant. My only contribution has been money, but yours has been much more."

"Hardly ninety-two thousand dollars' worth."

"Everything that's special and unique about this place is your doing. You conceived the idea, did the decorating, handled all the arrangements. It never would have happened without you."

"We can't possibly know that now, can we? You, in your infinite wisdom, decided to put the net under me. I'm right back where I started."

Jake tried to take her into his arms, but she wouldn't let herself be taken. She was confused and angry, and she had a right to be. But if she cared for him at all, she wouldn't leave now. "Don't be silly. Think of all you've accomplished." His arms swept the room. "This place is yours. I'm yours. I love you, Red, you can't deny that."

She only looked at him, and when he saw some of the fight go out of her, he pursued the subject. "It's only money. Something as meaningless as that shouldn't come between two people who love each other. It doesn't have to matter, I'll work the rest of my life to make it up to you."

Still she was silent.

"Don't you understand? I only wanted to take care of you, to protect you from hurt. Does that make me such an ogre?" Never in his life had Jake felt less sure of himself. He feared that he wasn't getting through to her at all. He wasn't doing a good job of convincing her that while his methods might have been wrong, his motives weren't.

"You just don't see, do you?" she asked in disbelief. How could he claim to love her and yet understand so little? "I've been telling you all along. I want to learn to take care of myself. I have no desire to be taken care of by you or anyone else."

He crossed the room and pulled her into his arms. She resisted, but he gave her no chance of escape. "And what of your desire for me? Have you none of that left either?"

She struggled against the conflicting emotions warring within her. She wanted his touch and hated herself for it. "The man I thought I loved would never have betrayed me the way you did."

"Betrayed you?" There was a desperate edge to his voice. "I thought I explained all that. I was wrong, I was stupid, I was insensitive. I should be horsewhipped or run out of town on a rail. Hanging is too good for me, but for God's sake, Red, don't stop loving me. That's one punishment I couldn't bear."

"Very dramatic, Jake. And I'm sure there are many women of your acquaintance to whom such a display would appeal. But I believe what we have here fits into the irreconcilable-differences category and we'd both be better off to admit it."

"I won't admit any such thing. Marry me."

"What?" she asked incredulously.

"Marry me. Tonight. Right now. There's no waiting period here, and even a notary public can conduct the ceremony. A woman has every right to accept help, financial and otherwise, from her husband. What about it?"

"You're crazy, and you're not listening. I can't marry you now. Don't you know me at all?"

"I, I! Me, me! Are you the only one you ever think about? All I know is I love you more than I ever thought it possible to love a woman. I know I'm willing to change, to do anything to make you forgive me."

"Nothing you can do will change my mind."

"That's pretty final." Jake was filled with what he felt was righteous indignation. April had no business to be so upset over a mistake that he had already admitted to and apologized for. What did she want? He couldn't, wouldn't grovel.

"Yes, it is."

"For the last time, is there anything I can do to make this up to you?" He couldn't talk to her when she had her back up like this. He'd have to give her time to cool off.

"Nothing. Just give it up, Jake. It won't work." She slipped away from him and started for the door. She had to get away from here before he changed her mind.

"It would if we made it work," he called after her, willing her to come back.

"It's too late," she said without turning around. "This kind of hurt can't be patched up with promises and kisses."

CHAPTER TEN

DURING THE NEXT week and a half, April avoided Jake whenever she could. She refused to answer his many phone calls and enlisted a reluctant Staci to turn him away at the door. Because of the girls' friendship, the clean break she would have preferred was impossible, and both of the children were devastated by their parents' unhappiness.

She tried to explain that while they could no longer be a foursome, she wanted the girls to feel free to continue their own relationship. Staci sulked in her room and refused to accept her mother's explanations. She blamed April for everything, and for the first time, an air of tension developed between them.

"Jake wants all of us to be together, he wants us to be a family. Molly told me so," Staci said one night when April entered her room to comfort her.

"I understand how you feel, darling, but we just can't be."

"We could if you'd forgive Jake for spending his money on you. You always tell me nothing is worth losing a friend over."

She had taken Staci into her arms and they'd cried together. The child because she was hurt and confused, the woman because she knew the child was right. She'd missed Jake more than one person had a right to miss another, and once her anger over his deception had dissipated, she'd been filled with despair. Although part of her understood that Jake had only been trying to help her, another part condemned him for it. Before long, she'd convinced herself that his interference was a result of his lack of faith in her, an attempt to control her life because he thought she was unable to do it herself. All she had now was her pride to keep her company, and pride, she soon learned, made a bitter companion.

The closer the date for the grand-opening party came, the worse she felt. Jake had gone on with the plans she had initiated, and she wondered how he could possibly celebrate when she herself felt so terrible. Either his feelings had not been as deep as he'd claimed, or he was already getting over her. She could only hope that her own heart would soon begin the healing process.

But the world wasn't content to let her do that. During the last week, she'd had a number of calls generated by a tacky article in a local scandal sheet. The callers wanted to know if she would care to comment on the rumors that her torrid affair with Jake Keegan was somehow linked to his recent decision to retire. Furious at the invasion of her privacy, she had hung up on them.

When the curious reporters began hanging around her building, hoping to get an interview, she finally admitted that she would need Jake's help to get rid of them. Wondering if perhaps she might possess masochistic tendencies for ever getting involved with him in the first place, she dialed Jake's number and waited with trepidation for him to answer.

"Jake, it's April." She took a deep breath, willing herself to remain calm.

"I know who you are, Red," he said softly. "It hasn't been that long." After nearly two heartbreaking weeks since he'd had so much as a glimpse of her, the sound of her voice wrenched at his emotions. Nearly two weeks without a word, and then she calls out of the blue. Don't hope for too much, he told himself.

His quiet words, unaccusing and gentle, encouraged the tears she was fighting. Stalling until she could regain control, she inquired after Staci, who had spent the night with the Keegans. "Are the girls giving you any trouble?"

"Yeah. They keep suggesting ways for me to make things up to you. Crawling on my hands and knees and begging forgiveness was their most recent idea. You know what? I'm seriously contemplating it."

"Don't, Jake."

"Okay, I won't. Have you talked to Chaz and Ivy lately?"

"Yes, Ivy called me when she got her test results. They really want this baby, and I'm so happy for them."

"Me, too. It's nice to know that some dreams do come true." He had a sudden, unbidden image of what a child of his and April's might look like and quickly dashed the thought.

"Jake, we need to talk," she said in a voice too shaky to suit her.

"Yes, we do," he agreed quickly. "Among other things. Name the time and place."

April recognized the unconcealed eagerness in his tone and realized that she was just as anxious to see him. "What I want to talk to you about has nothing to do with a reconciliation, so don't jump to any conclusions."

"No, there's been enough of that done already." Jake leaned back in his chair, closed his eyes, and gripped the receiver. "What exactly does it have to do with?"

"Another little problem." It was hard to force the words around the lump of tears in her throat. "I'd rather discuss it without the girls around. Would you be willing to come over here?"

"I'll be there in ten minutes."

"Jake?"

"Yes?"

"Be careful of the reporters."

"What reporters?" he asked the dial tone.

When Jake arrived, there were three or four men milling around in front of April's building. He recognized them as local news hounds and chided them about not having anything more important to investigate.

"But this is important, Jake. The paper's been getting calls from concerned sports fans about your sudden retirement. All kinds of rumors have been circulating, and we're just trying to get to the truth, that's all."

Jake's look let them know he recognized bull when he heard it. "Yeah, and inquiring minds want to know, right?" He ignored the rest of their questions and pounded on April's door. Once inside, he leaned against it, taking time to drink in the sight of her.

"God, I've missed you, Red."

April's heart turned over when she saw the raw pain reflected in his eyes. She tried not to respond to him, but she couldn't stop the words. "I've missed you too, Jake."

"Then what are you doing way over there?" He held out his arms and prayed she would step into them. "Come here."

"I can't."

His long legs closed the distance between them. "Well, hell, I can." He saw her hesitation and knew that although she wanted the embrace, she wouldn't let herself have it.

April wheeled away from him. "Please, Jake. Don't make this any harder than it already is."

He stalked over to the window and looked out at the reporters, who waved a friendly greeting. "What's going on?"

Her heart still pounding from his nearness, April scooped up a local scandal sheet she had picked up in the supermarket. "It seems that your little friend Gretchen told it all, as they say." She paced the room, slapping her thigh with the paper. "What did you do to her to make her vindictive enough to want to publicize the intimate details of your life?"

Jake gave her the barest hint of his one-sided grin. Making himself comfortable on the sofa, he began, "I think it was what I didn't do to her that made her mad. I had one date with her, which ended rather badly. I walked out on her in a night club when she trotted out her drug paraphernalia." He smiled at her innocently. "I followed everyone's advice. I just said no."

"She did that in public?" April asked incredulously.

"She did," he confirmed.

"And you just left her there?"

"Ungallant of me, I'll admit. But at the time, it was all I could do to keep from wringing her neck."

"Good. She could have gotten you into all kinds of trouble."

"I'm glad you finally approve of something I did."

"Have you read this?" She tossed him the paper.

"No. And frankly, I'm surprised that you did. This thing is trash."

"Trash it may be, but it's highly quotable trash. The headline reads 'EVERYONE'S FAVORITE RAKE STRIKES AGAIN.'" She went on to quote the article: "'Florida's own Jake Keegan isn't content to confine his scoring to the basketball court.'" April tossed him the paper and slumped into a chair. "Read on. It gets worse."

Jake read aloud: "'The Rake told a reliable source that he met his current ladylove, April Conway, when he saved her from a Jacksonville jail cell. When this reporter tried to confirm the story, the authorities said no one by that name had been arrested. However, several police officers admitted that the Rake had been in the station a few weeks earlier and had left with someone matching Ms. Conway's description.

"'This news comes on the heels of Keegan's recent announcement of his retirement. Is the Rake in danger of becoming domesticated at last? If so, basketball will be a mite tame in these parts from now on. Not only will we lose his expertise on the court, but also his exploits off it. It's hard to say which one his fans will miss the most.'"

Jake hooted and tossed the paper on the coffee table. "So? What's the big deal?"

"I'll tell you. I got a call from Fred Phariss, saying I could pick up my new car, and I can't even leave the house to go get it. Those reporters out there want my side of the story."

"Why don't you give it to them?"

"Jake! I can't believe you're taking this invasion of your privacy so calmly."

Jake chuckled. "They've printed a lot worse. Even the people who read the stuff don't take it seriously."

"I don't know how you can laugh about it. They printed my *name* in the paper and implied awful things about us."

"Awful? Let me see that again." He reached for the paper. "I thought it said we were in love."

"That's not what it meant. If Caleb's parents were to get a hold of this, I'd never hear the end of it."

"This is a local rag, and those are only local sports reporters outside. Or did I miss the national ones?"

"Jake, will you be serious for once in your life?" His nonchalance over a matter that made April see red only frustrated her further.

"I was serious about you, and what good did it do me?" The look he leveled at her was so intense, April could feel the heat of it across the small living room.

"What about the reporters?" she asked.

"I have a feeling they're more interested in my retirement than in my love life."

"Then why are they hanging around in front of my apartment?"

"I don't know. Why don't we go out there and ask them? Calm down, Red. Everything will be okay."

"You'd better hope so," she warned.

"Hey, don't blame this on me. You're the one who

popped off and gave dear Gretchen the fuel she needed. If you hadn't been in such a jealous snit, none of this would have happened."

"Jealous snit?" April jumped from her chair and glared up at him. "Jealous snit?"

"That's what I said."

"I was not jealous!" She wasn't sure whether her anger was due to righteous indignation or to having the truth pointed out so bluntly.

He gave her an amused look. "Sorry, my mistake."

"Don't you dare grin at me!"

"I can't believe you're so angry over this. It would expedite matters if you'd just admit that you're still upset about the restaurant."

"I won't deny that." April crossed her arms and paced the room.

"At the risk of repeating myself, I'll admit that you had every right to be thoroughly infuriated, but only for ten, maybe fifteen, minutes."

"Ten or fifteen minutes?"

"That's right. After that, reason, logic, and love should have set in to make you realize I did it only in your best interests." He pushed her gently down in a chair and bent over her, his hands gripping the arms of the chair. They were practically nose to nose when he said, "I was wrong, and I'm sorry, and I've paid a dear price. So how much longer are you going to punish both of us with this standoff?"

Her gaze was drawn to the promise in his eyes, the softness of his lips. "Forever."

"I don't believe you mean that. I can't."

"Believe it. I can be pretty stubborn."

"This isn't a contest, it's our future. All I did was to care too much too soon. If loving you is a crime, then I'm as guilty as a man can be . . . because heart and soul, I love you, Red."

April strained back against the cushions, trying to keep

the emotions he aroused within her from taking over. "I don't believe that, Jake. In the beginning, I was a challenge because I disapproved of you and you knew it. You couldn't bear the thought that any female could resist you, so you set out to make me fall in love with you."

"You've got it all wrong, Red. I didn't set out to do anything. It just happened."

"Maybe so," she conceded. "But that doesn't change the fact that you went behind my back and bought the restaurant out from under me."

"I bought it *for* you! I thought we had a future together and I wanted . . . never mind. You know the truth, and all the talking in the world won't make any difference. You're determined not to understand."

"I understand. I just can't accept."

Jake made one last attempt. "What if we were married and you decided to buy a business? Wouldn't you expect your husband to support you financially as well as emotionally?"

"But we're not married."

"But if we were?" he insisted.

"I suppose so, but—"

"That settles it. We'll get married and you can consider the restaurant a wedding gift."

"Stop it, Jake. Do you think getting married would make it all just go away?"

"It could if you'd let go of it." He pulled her from the chair and into his arms.

April put her hands against his chest in a token protest. But she didn't try too hard to push him away. "Maybe in time I can."

"That's the best news I've had all day. I'm glad you're willing to make a start. But then, I knew that when you called me over here. You didn't need me to shoo away a few harmless reporters. You had an ulterior motive, and I know what it was," he said, his lips just a hairbreadth away.

"Why shouldn't you? You know everything."

"Hardly. But when it comes to my feelings for you, I do. I know you better than you know yourself."

"I'd rather not hear about that."

"Too bad, you're going to." Gently he took her hands in his, and his voice softened. "I paid that damned money hoping it would give me time to show you what a swell guy I am, what a great team we'd make."

She turned her head aside when his lips would have covered hers. "You should have asked me first. That's all it would have taken."

"Would you have agreed?"

"No."

"That's what I thought. How about this? Pay me back. Write me a check every month," he breathed against her cheek. "Will that satisfy your sense of independence?"

"No, it isn't the same thing," she murmured. "Let me go, Jake."

He released her. "Go," he said huskily. "I can't stop you, no matter how much I want to. Walk away from me if you can."

April couldn't, she didn't want to. When his lips brushed her ear, her knees threatened to desert her and she flung her arms around his neck. "Why are you doing this?"

"Because I'm a desperate man, and because you have enough pride for both of us," he muttered against her hair. "You can reject my love, but you can't deny that your body craves mine. Make love with me, Red," he pleaded as their lips met.

April allowed herself the pleasure of kissing him back lightly, then wrenched away. "You know I want you. If you kiss me again, I won't be able to turn you away. If you're trying to prove your power over me, you've succeeded. But it'll be a hollow victory."

Jake took her hand in his. "Don't do this to us, Red."

"I don't know anything anymore, Jake." She squeezed

his fingers. "When we're this close, I can't sort things out. I just don't know what I should do."

"We'll let it rest and talk about it later. Okay?"

His eyes pleaded with her, and she had never seen him so unsure of himself. The need she saw tied her heart in knots, and she could only nod.

The relief Jake felt was nearly overwhelming. She was beginning to understand, to come around. "Are you coming to the grand-opening party tonight? Several local dignitaries have rsvp-ed, and it promises to be a black-tie blowout."

She pulled her hand away from his. "I don't think so. It's your investment. It's your grand opening, not mine."

"Nonsense. You paid for all the renovations and supplies. You set up this shindig: all I did was mail the invitations. Please come."

"I don't think I can. I'm sorry, Jake." She refused to look at him.

"Me, too, Red," he sighed. He opened the door and stepped out into the group of persistent reporters.

April watched in dismay as a local camera crew joined the throng. Why couldn't everyone just leave them alone? She saw Jake shake hands with the man holding the microphone and smile amiably into the camera. They spoke for a few moments and then the newsman gestured at her door. Jake's answer must have been funny, because everyone laughed. After a few more seconds of conversation, he seemed to appeal to the heavens and earned another laugh. He waved his hands in a "that's it, folks" gesture, and one by one the news people began to leave, having apparently gotten the story they had come for.

She went into her bedroom and indulged in a fit of tears and self-recrimination. She had handled things badly; she should have been firmer with Jake. She shouldn't have given him any encouragement. It was easy to think like this when he was gone, but oh, so difficult to do when he was holding her. Maybe she was hurting now, but it was better not to continue their relationship. She might not be able to endure another deception.

She would get over him in time, all she had to do was to forget how he looked when he grinned at her. To forget the way his lips felt on hers and the feel of his body against her own. To forget the way he made the simplest outing fun and exciting, the way he had of making her laugh when she didn't want to. She took a deep breath and knew that even if she made it her life's work, she would never forget Jake Keegan. Never in a million years.

She dozed fitfully and a short time later was awakened by the doorbell. When she answered it, she was surprised to see Conchata and the girls standing there, their faces filled with hopeful expectation, their arms filled with gifts.

Conchata carried three boxes of long-stemmed roses into the living room. "Meester Jake say to breeng you roses. I say what color? And he say whatever meens love. And I say—"

Molly interrupted, "Pops wanted you to know he loves you, April, that's all."

Staci placed a candy box in her mother's arms. "This yummy, giant-size box of designer chocolates is yours, too." Without asking permission, she lifted the lid and popped a chocolate caramel into her mouth.

"What's going on here?" April demanded.

"You two didn't do so good at patching things up today, so we thought we'd help things along," Molly explained.

"Thank you for your concern, but this is between your father and me. It has nothing to do with you girls."

"But it does," Staci insisted quietly. "Jake loves us, too, and he told Molly and me that he wants to marry us but that you don't want to."

"Baby, there's more to it than that."

"Mom, you always told me that nothing I could ever do would make you stop loving me. Don't you love Jake enough to forgive him?"

April looked at her daughter with tears in her eyes. "The

relationship between a man and woman is different from that of a mother and child, darling. I love you unconditionally and without qualifications. You can't understand that now, but I hope someday you will."

"I won't ever understand. We were so happy, and Molly and I were almost like real sisters. It's not fair. You never told me there were different kinds of love."

"I'm sorry, honey."

"But what good is love if it isn't unconditional?" asked Molly. "That's like saying 'I'll only love you as long as you make it easy for me to.' That's not what love is supposed to be."

"Molly's right, Mom. The only kind of love worth having is the real kind. If you loved Jake once, really truly loved him, you can't stop just because he made a mistake, can you?"

April looked at the children in amazement. It was true, that old saying about wisdom coming from the mouths of babes. The problem between herself and Jake was a complicated matter of misguided motives, doubts, and insecurities, but the girls had reduced it to its common denominator: love. To them, if you loved someone, that was enough.

Maybe adults would be better off, maybe the whole world would be a happier place to live in if only everyone viewed life as straightforwardly and honestly as children did. How could she claim to love Jake and then let something as intrinsically worthless as pride keep her from admitting that he had paid for the restaurant because he cared, not because he had any desire to hurt or dominate her?

Jake was accustomed to solving problems in the most expedient way, and his generosity was one of the things she most admired about him. So why did she reject it when it was turned upon her?

"Sometimes adults can be so childish," Molly put in.

"You're always telling us kids to say 'I'm sorry' and

make up," Staci accused. "But grown-ups can't even do it themselves."

"You're messing with our future," Molly told her. "Oh, I know Staci and I can still be like sisters even if you two don't get married. But what about Pops? He might not get over this. He had tears in his eyes when he told us you wouldn't come to the party tonight."

Conchata, who had remained silent during the exchange, sniffed and dabbed at her eyes. "Meester Jake ees so broken down, it's about to hurt my heart," she confirmed.

"That's broken *up*, Conchata," Molly clarified.

April sighed. "I have a feeling that this is some kind of trick. Jake didn't send you over here with this stuff, did he? Come on, confession builds character."

"He would have if he'd thought of it," defended Molly.

"We had to do something," Staci told her. "You two have let this thing get ridiculous."

Remembering the clear plastic box in her hand, Molly held it out to April. "Here, Pops wanted me to give you this. Really," she insisted at April's skeptical look.

April opened the corsage box and inside was an engraved invitation to the party. Her breath caught when she read the message scrawled in Jake's bold hand across the cream vellum: "*I wait for redheads.*"

She set the box of orchids on the coffee table and pulled the girls down to sit beside her on the sofa. With an arm around each of them, she said with tears in her eyes, "You two little schemers. You really know how to cut through the nonsense, don't you?"

"Especially when it's grown-up nonsense," Molly said.

April hugged the girls and felt better than she had in days. Nothing was worth losing Jake. Nothing was worth risking the future happiness of four people. Jake had said that independence was a state of being that came from within. He had been as right as his daughter had been. Independence was freedom of choice, and April felt immense relief that she no longer had to carry the burden of her pride.

She was free to choose, and she chose love.

"Don't worry, girls." She gave them each a kiss. "You've given me more insight in the last ten minutes than I would have gained in ten years on my own. Thanks."

"Does this mean everything's going to be all right?" Staci asked.

"It means I'm going to try to make everything all right." They clung together, and laughed and cried a little.

Conchata glanced at her watch and remarked nervously, "I hate to interrupt thees tender moment, but we do not have much time." She pointed meaningfully at the television set in the corner.

"Time for what?" April asked.

Molly jumped up, switched on the set, and tuned in to the six-o'clock news.

"We must watch the sports, how you call it. Jockumentary?"

"Commentary," Staci offered helpfully.

"What's so important?" April sensed that there was more to the conspiracy that had brought Conchata and the girls here in the first place, but she felt so happy that she didn't mind being manipulated.

"It ees a mystery. Meester Jake tell me not to ask any more questions when I geeve him a message, so I am forced to listen on the extension when he call thees Brad person back. He tell Meester Jake to watch the news. Ooooh, look, there he ees now."

Jake's image filled the screen, and April's heart tripled its beat at the sight of him. The camera swooped to the familiar-looking commentator who had waylaid Jake earlier in front of her apartment.

"Hello, I'm Brad Payton, and I'm visiting with Jake Keegan, better known to all you basketball fans as Jake the Rake. Tell us, Jake, are the rumors true?"

Jake grinned. "It must be a slow news day, huh? But to

answer your question, Brad, that depends on the rumor. Could you be more specific?"

"Are you really leaving basketball? And if so, why?"

"I am, and because it's time."

"Come on, Jake. You've got a lot of fans out there who are going to be very disappointed when they hear this. We're all going to miss you."

"I'll probably miss them, too, but what better time to retire than when you're on top?"

"What are your plans now?"

"I'm in the restaurant business," Jake confided. Never one to miss free publicity, he gave the address and other pertinent information.

"Will we be hearing wedding bells soon, Jake? There's a rumor circulating that you've found a lady you're pretty serious about."

"The way rumors get around, are you sure we need you guys?" Jake smiled beguilingly into the camera and winked.

"Would this by any chance be the home of April Conway, the lady you met when you allegedly bailed her out of jail?"

"I've never bailed a lady out of jail in my life. April and I met through our daughters."

"Then you aren't romantically involved with Miss Conway?"

"I didn't say that."

Brad was good at reading between the lines. "So there's truth to the rumor after all?"

"For once. I'm in so deep, I'm up to my eyeballs."

Brad looked astounded. "This is a scoop! Jake the Rake has a real, live significant other? Whatever happened to the man who once told me and anyone who cared to listen that freedom, next to his daughter, was his most important possession?"

Jake looked up directly in the camera. "He fell in love."

April wiped happy tears from her eyes and lost track of

the rest of the conversation. How dare he go on television and announce to the world that he loved her? Maybe he'd staged this whole thing for her benefit. Well, he had wasted his time. She'd known it all along.

Conchata turned off the television and April took the girls' hands in hers. "Staci, how would you feel about having Jake for a father?" She wanted to be absolutely sure of her daughter's feelings.

"I loved Daddy, Mom, but he's gone forever, isn't he?"

"Yes, baby, he is."

"I think Daddy would want us to marry Jake."

April brushed Staci's hair with her lips. "I think so, too, baby. I think so, too."

April turned to Molly, who didn't wait for the question before supplying her own answer. "I told Pops I thought you'd make a great mom for me." She grinned up at April. "I mean, we already like each other, and you've got experience and wouldn't quit on me when the going got tough. Not that it will, but you never know about these things."

Conchata jumped to her feet in excitement. "Does thees meen there weel be a wedding after all? I weel make the cake. I just love weddings!"

April laughed. "Don't start baking yet, Conchata. I have a few things to make up to Jake."

Molly and Staci were doing a little jig, and April was forced to put two fingers in her mouth to whistle for silence. "I have a plan, and you girls can help by going with Conchata to the opening party tonight. Don't say a word to Jake about my coming. I want the element of surprise on my side. Then go straight home with Conchata afterward. Jake and I have some talking to do, and some unfinished business to take care of."

"Ah, is that all we get to do?" Staci asked with a frown.

"No." Molly, who was more worldly than her friend, nudged Staci in the ribs. "We can help by staying out of their way."

"That's right. Give us a little time to straighten things out. Okay?"

"Okay," they chimed.

After Conchata left with the girls, April prepared for what promised to be the most important evening of her life. She appraised the results of her primping in the mirror and decided that her hair and makeup looked more exotic than normal. But she was lotioned and perfumed to perfection, and the gown she had purchased for the opening was very sexy. It was a long sheath of black which molded her curves and showed them to advantage. The long, tight sleeves were banded with tiny strips of rhinestones, as were the slit back of the long skirt and the mock-turtleneck collar. This was one daring outfit, and she hoped she looked as good in it as it made her feel.

In fact, she felt downright lascivious and decided to throw caution to the wind and wear the gift that Conchata had pulled from her tote bag and pressed upon her as she left. Conchata had told her that it was something new and blue for good luck. Conchata's taste in lingerie was scandalous, but April was the only one who would know that the lacy bra was adorned with tiny whistles.

Her bid for glamour had taken more of April's time than she could afford without arriving too late to be fashionable. She jumped into the sporty demo and screeched out of the drive and into the flow of nighttime traffic. No one else seemed to be in a hurry and she maueuvered her way impatiently among the more sedate drivers, finally passing all of them.

With open road ahead and the wind in her hair, April pressed her foot down hard on the gas pedal and the Mustang zoomed through the balmy tropical night, rushing her toward Jake and happiness. Everything would be all right. They loved each other. What could be simpler? Nothing could stand in their way now.

A loud siren penetrated April's thoughts, and she instinctively let up on the gas and glanced in the rearview mirror to see what the trouble was. There was no mistaking the flashing red-and-blue lights of the patrol car behind her. Frustrated that her own stupidity had caused what would be a maddening delay, she pulled onto the shoulder and braked.

She picked up her beaded bag and rummaged inside for her driver's license. Holding it out to the approaching patrolman, she said, "I guess I was speeding, officer, but tonight is special and I was running late." She smiled up at his scowling face and hoped he would skip the lecture and just give her the ticket so she could be on her way.

The officer shone his flashlight in her face, then at the license. He handed it to his partner, a young rookie, to check it out, and April waited impatiently for the younger man to return. She had to endure pleasantries with the older cop while they waited.

"Look, officer, I know I was speeding. Can you just give me my ticket, please?"

The rookie stepped up at that moment and gave the other policeman a knowing look. "We don't give tickets for driving stolen vehicles, ma'am." The flashlight shone in her face again and she blinked. "That's a felony."

"Stolen car?" April's words echoed the rookie's. "This isn't a stolen car. It's borrowed."

The cops exchanged smug looks and the younger one had the gall to smirk. "That's what they all say."

"Mrs. Conway." The polite partner touched the brim of his hat. "I'm afraid you're going to have to come along with us."

"But I didn't steal the car," she protested.

The rookie intoned in a formal voice, "You have the right to remain silent..."

CHAPTER ELEVEN

"SERGEANT SANDUSKY!" April recognized a familiar face in the noisy police station and was never so happy to see anyone in her life. She glared at the two patrolmen who had done their duty by bringing her in for questioning despite her explanations and her protests of innocence. "Tell these officers I'm not a car thief," she said after the three had conferred.

The burly desk sergeant grinned. "You seem to have your share of car trouble, Mrs. Conway." He turned to the men and explained. "The last time she was here, it was *her* car that was stolen."

"Does she have a record?" According to the bar pinned to his chest, the overzealous rookie's name was Yates. "Want me to run a check on her, Sarge?"

April couldn't believe this was happening. How many more times would she have to explain? "Of course I don't have a record." Yet, she added silently. Given the mood she was in and the rookie's refusal to listen to reason, her chances of being charged with felonious assault were increasing by the minute. "There's been some kind of mistake."

April waited for the ever-ready Yates to utter the time-honored line she had heard in a dozen cop films: "Yeah, and you're the one who made it, buddy." Instead, he prodded, "But you did take the car?"

"I didn't 'take it' in the sense you mean. Fred Phariss himself gave me that car to drive until the one I ordered came in. You've heard of Fred, haven't you?" She proceeded to sing the lyrics of the car dealer's jingle from his do-it-yourself television commercials. "Come on down to Fred Phariss Ford . . . he's got a fine deal waiting for you."

When she finished, she noticed that the three men were looking at her like they had just seen her face on a wanted poster. "It's a mistake, I tell you. An oversight."

Sandusky rifled through some papers. "How long have you had the car, Mrs. Conway?"

"About four weeks." They looked skeptical. "My car has been on back-order." They still looked skeptical. "I can't help it if the automotive industry is slow," she defended.

Yates, who had been reading over the sergeant's shoulder, looked up triumphantly. "Four weeks, huh? That's how long it's been reported stolen."

April glared at him and then at the other two, whose joint amusement was not helping matters. "I know you are determined to charge me with auto theft, but may I raise a point? Since I've been driving that car around on city streets for four weeks, how come it took so long for Jacksonville's finest to apprehend me?—an obviously wanton and dangerous criminal." She glanced at her watch and gasped in dismay. The grand-opening party was well underway by now. She regretted having made the girls promise not to tell Jake her plans. It might be hours before she could let him know she had changed her mind about the restaurant, about him, and about their future.

"No need to get hostile, lady," Yates said in his most officious tone. "We got lucky this time. Usually when a professional steals from a dealership, it's for the purpose of selling to order, and the cars are never recovered."

"Professional!" She was getting nowhere with this guy so she turned to Sandusky and the heretofore silent partner. "Hey, I can't even break into my own car when I lock the keys inside. Besides, if I was the expert he," she indicated Yates with a toss of her head, "claims I am, would I be driving around with the dealer's tag on the back?"

Sergeant Sandusky stifled a laugh, the older cop glanced at the ceiling, but the rookie felt compelled to answer what she had meant as a purely rhetorical question. "The criminal mind works in strange ways. That's what makes this job so fascinating."

April could only stare at him in astonishment. "Sergeant Sandusky," she asked through clenched teeth, "how long would I get for assaulting an officer?"

The sergeant didn't stifle his laugh this time. "Now, now, Mrs. Conway, don't get all worked up. I'm sure this is all some kind of misunderstanding that can be resolved soon."

"How soon?"

"Soon," he evaded.

She looked at her watch again. "I can spare fifteen minutes tops. Then I have to be out of here."

"Sorry, but the criminal justice system doesn't work quite that fast." Sandusky sent the patrolmen away to write up their report and Yates glanced at her over his shoulder as if he fully expected her to attempt a daring daylight jailbreak.

April surveyed the crowded station. "What's going on, Sergeant? Are you running a get-busted-for-half-price special?"

"The guys from vice conducted an early raid tonight. There's always a bunch of reporters nosing around trying to make a story out of nothing."

When she noticed that most of those being detained were women, April quickly realized what kind of raid it had been.

"Since we're kind of busy right now, just come with

me, Mrs. Conway, and I'll show you to the holding cell."

April stared at him in disbelief. The man acted as if he were about to escort her to her room at the Hilton. "Wait a minute. I watch TV. I'm entitled to a phone call."

"Of course you are." The sergeant pointed the way to a pay phone situated just outside a large cell populated by milling women. He handed her a coin with instructions to keep it brief.

April considered for a moment before dropping the quarter into the slot. She wasn't likely to reach Fred Phariss at the dealership at this hour, and if someone were there, it would probably be the same idiot who had reported the car stolen in the first place. She didn't know Phariss's home number, and she didn't have an attorney. That left only one choice. The only real choice. Jake.

She dialed the restaurant and the phone rang several times before the new bartender answered. She waited interminably for Jake to take the call, the sergeant tapping impatiently on his watch the whole time. How was she going to explain the need to be rescued from jail a second time? Jake was going to love this!

When she heard his familiar voice, she decided to dispense with opening statements and simply plead her case. "Jake, can you come and get me?"

"Red? Where are you?"

She sighed. This was the part he would enjoy. "In jail."

"I didn't hear all of that. Did you say at or in?"

"I said in."

"In?" His calm voice infuriated her. "In as in arrested?"

Did she detect a hint of smugness in that question? "That's right. In, as in properly Mirandized, as in awaiting booking. As in guilty until proven innocent."

Jake was quiet for a few moments. Then, in a curious voice, he asked, "What exactly did you do?"

"I didn't do anything. They say I stole the demo, but that's absurd since you were with me when that weasel Phariss handed me the keys. Look, Jake, you have to come down here and corroborate my story, use your influence. They'll believe Jake the Rake."

"I thought you disapproved of celebrity privilege."

"I do, in theory. I also disapprove of food preservatives, but since they're so pervasive in our society, I'm learning to live with them."

Jake's chuckle did nothing to improve her attitude. "Could you learn to live with me?"

"Jake, will you be serious? You don't seem to understand the gravity of the situation." She whispered into the mouthpiece. "They're going to put me in a cell. With..." She looked around and wondered how the ladies referred to themselves. She didn't want to offend anyone. "There was a raid and..." She noticed Nadia and Bootsy in one corner, and the two women waved in recognition. "This cell is full of..."

"Working girls," Nadia called out helpfully.

April acknowledged the information with a wan smile. "Jake, there's a gung-ho cop here who's made it his personal mission to send me to Alcatraz."

"They don't send people to Alcatraz anymore. It's been closed for years."

"Stop it!" She looked up and saw that the sergeant was more impatient than ever. "This is the only phone call I get to make, and you're wasting it on idle chatter."

"You used your one phone call on me?" His voice lowered and she knew he had that seductive grin on his face. The one that always made her forget her good intentions. "That really makes me feel wanted."

"I'm warning you, Jake." She didn't go on. She knew he was teasing. The banter was his own special style of perverse pay-back. He was still upset over her stubborn refusal to accept his help. Wasn't she practically begging for it now? "I guess I should have called a lawyer. I'm sure he would have been more help."

"Help?" Jake pretended incredulity. "Is it possible that

the independent April Conway actually needs the help of a buttinsky jerk like Jake Keegan?"

"Yes." Her answer was simple because it was the simple truth. She did need him. She needed him a lot.

"I don't know. You told me you didn't want to be helped or taken care of. That you wanted to do everything yourself."

"Things have changed," she admitted softly.

"Have they, now? You mean you've discovered that independence is a team sport? That you can allow yourself to be loved and still be a rugged individualist?"

"Have I refused to allow myself to be loved?" April hadn't thought of it in just those terms.

"That's exactly what you've done. Damn it, I know you can take care of yourself. I know you could live a perfectly fulfilled life without me. But why do you have to when I'm offering my love and protection? Till death do us part."

April felt close to tears. Why had she been so stubborn? Why had she denied all that Jake meant to her? God, she had been ready to give him up, ready to give up on both of them. "I don't have to, Jake," she said with a catch in her voice. "And I don't want to. I love you."

She thought she heard him breathe a sigh of relief. "That's what I wanted to hear. I love you, too, Red."

His words made her heart pound, and she closed her eyes for a second so the wondrous sound of them could echo in her mind. When she opened her eyes, she saw a stern visage. "Jake, Sergeant Sandusky is scowling at me. I think my time's up."

Jake laughed, and in that one sound she heard a thousand promises for the future. "That's where you're wrong, Red. Your time is just beginning." He assured her that he would be there as soon as possible and hung up.

April sat on a bench inside the cell, and Nadia plopped down beside her. Her hair was still pink. "Small world, kid. What would you say the odds of us ever meeting again were? And in jail, no less. What are you in for this time?"

April's thoughts were still on Jake. Everything was going to work out. It had to. "Grand theft, auto."

"Whoa!" Bootsy sat down on the other side of her. "Now that's what I call a career move."

"Despite opinion to the contrary, I have not embarked on a life of crime. It's all a horrible mistake."

The two women looked at each other knowingly. "Right, you was framed. Weren't we all?"

April groaned and put her head in her hands. This was hardly the way she'd planned to spend the evening. Judging by what he'd said on the telephone, the reconciliation with Jake was going to be easier than she'd thought; she could hardly wait for him to get here so she could feel his arms around her again. He had been right about her, right about everything. She had behaved like an insecure fool. Thankfully, he'd been smart enough not to take her too seriously.

If he had obeyed her wishes, there wouldn't be a grand-opening party tonight, because there would be no restaurant. There would be no Jake. No love to end all loves. He'd only been wrong about one thing: He had said she could have a perfectly fulfilled life without him.

She wanted to sit in silence and reflect on the past and, more important, plan for the future. But Nadia and Bootsy seemed determined to make the most of their reunion and filled her in on all the details of the raid.

"Damned exciting, as far as raids go," Nadia allowed.

"Best-looking vice cops I've seen since Don Johnson," Bootsy agreed.

"That rumpled-looking one was really giving you the eye, Boots."

Now it was April's turn to laugh in spite of the gravity of the situation. Here they were, awaiting booking in a holding cell, and Nadia and Bootsy were discussing the policemen who'd arrested them in the same manner other women discussed encounters in singles' bars.

"How can you make light of this?" April asked them between giggles. "You're in jail."

"Jail?" Nadia asked with feigned surprise. "Why the hell didn't somebody tell me?"

"Yeah," Bootsy said. "We thought this home away from home was a Girl Scout camp."

"If it's jail, shouldn't we be rattling the bars with tin cups or something?" Nadia's guffaw was deep and resonant.

April laughed again at their antics. "Aren't you worried about what will happen to you?"

"Nah. We'll be out of here in no time. Don't worry, kid, It's a piece of cake."

They acted nonchalant enough, but April was no less amazed by their attitude. They regaled her with stories about some of their escapades, and soon they were all laughing and giggling like sorority girls at a pajama party. The other occupants of the cell must have thought they were either drunk or crazy, because most of them moved to the opposite side and watched them suspiciously.

Jake arrived with Staci, Molly, Fred Phariss, and Judge Henry Bates in tow. Lucky for him, the district judge and Phariss had accepted his invitation to the grand-opening bash. Lucky also that despite his lofty office, the judge had a sense of humor and had agreed to accompany Jake on his matrimonial mission.

Phariss spoke to the sergeant on duty and quickly cleared April of all suspicion. He had forgotten to tell the computer, or any one else for that matter, that he had loaned out the car. A conscientious employee had followed the proper procedure and reported the vehicle stolen. A bit red-faced, the dealer said he was returning to the party, and Jake, the judge, and the girls were escorted back to April's cell.

Jake's breath caught when he saw April behind bars with a scruffy-looking collection of what she'd referred to as "working girls." Beautiful in a chic black dress and glamorous hairdo, she shone like a diamond in a tray of pebbles. How proud he was of her, how determined he was to make her his, how much he loved her.

"Visitors, Mrs. Conway," said the sergeant.

April was having so much fun with Nadia and Bootsy that she was unaware that nearly an hour had passed. When she saw who her visitors were, she rushed to the bars and thrust her hands out between them.

"I'm so glad to see you!" She hugged Staci and Molly, who had stepped up to take a look inside. "Get me out of here," she told Jake, who looked exactly as tuxedo tailors intended men to look in their creations.

"Whatsa matter, April? Don'cha like our company?" Bootsy asked with a grin.

April turned back to the two women. "It's been fun. I hope I see you both again."

"Yeah," Nadia teased. "Let's do lunch sometime. But not in here. Jail-house food is the pits."

"No, not in here. Good luck." The women smiled and wished her the same.

Sandusky moved to unlock the cell, but Jake had other ideas. "Not so fast there, Sergeant."

"What do you mean, 'not so fast'?" April demanded.

"I want to spring you, but there's a provision you'll have to agree to first. Judge Bates is here to make sure it's carried out."

April tried to protest, but he cut her off. "You're a captive audience, and you're going to hear what I have to say."

"Very well. Say it."

"I'm not about to risk losing you again, so you can't leave until you marry me."

"What! Here? In jail?"

"Judge Bates has issued us a license and is prepared to tie the knot," Jake explained. "All you have to do is say yes."

Molly and Staci giggled and the judge smiled. Sergeant

Sandusky beamed, and Nadia and Bootsy poked each other in the ribs.

"You must be kidding." Did he really think she would submit to such strong-arm tactics. "You took a lot upon yourself, didn't you?"

"You have to marry Jake, Mom," Staci put in. "Molly and I will never be real sisters unless you do."

"Not only that," Jake added, "but none of us will ever be happy unless you do."

"Not only that," put in Judge Bates, "but we're all missing a heckuva party at JAKE'S."

April was speechless. She'd already decided that Jake was the only man for her. She'd been fantasizing about their future together, about how the four of them would be a big, happy family. He didn't need to resort to coercion, she wanted to marry him. But she didn't say yes right away. Two could play at this game.

She turned to the policeman. "Sergeant, isn't this a blatant case of blackmail?"

"It could be called that," he admitted reluctantly.

"Just as I thought. Maybe I'd better call that attorney after all."

"Sorry, but you can't do that," Sandusky reminded her. "You already made the one phone call you're entitled to."

"Mom-om-om!" the girls voiced their dismay.

April smiled at Molly, who had also called her "Mom." This was going to work out just fine. She winked slyly at the girls to relieve their apparent anxiety. "I don't know. I'll have to think it over." She went back to the bench and sat down between Nadia and Bootsy.

"Are you crazy?" Nadia's expression indicated that she thought April was. "What's to think over already? The guy's gorgeous. He's handsome, he's tall, he's..." She looked at him more closely. "He's Jake the Rake!"

The other detainees rushed to the front of the cell to confirm Nadia's announcement, and there were murmurs of awe from among the women. April was amused to know that his recent retirement hadn't dimmed his star.

Jake acknowledged his fans with a smile and a nod. "Don't take too long, Red. You've got a restaurant full of people waiting for you. So far, the place has been a big hit. I think JAKE'S has a promising future."

The restaurant wasn't the only thing with a promising future. While she pretended to mull over Jake's proposal, several of her cell mates offered to take her place should she decide to reject it.

"A police station is not an ideal wedding chapel," she said, "and it might be bad luck to get married in black."

"I'll trade you clothes," Nadia offered.

April glanced at the woman's hot-pink mini-dress and declined the offer. "But I suppose stranger things have happened."

"Much stranger," Jake agreed. "I've heard of people getting married underwater, while free-falling from an airplane, on horseback, and in a hot-air balloon. Who's to say getting married in jail is strange?"

At about that time, the area outside the cell became crowded as reporters who'd come to cover the city-wide vice raid found a more interesting subject for their questions and cameras.

"Does your impending marriage have anything to do with your decision to retire?" asked a reporter.

"What's your lady in for?"

Jake answered their questions in the amiable way that had made him such a media favorite. He grinned and teased and posed for pictures and invited all of the reporters to join the party at JAKE'S.

"Your fans took the news of your retirement hard," pointed out a female reporter whose tongue was lodged firmly in her cheek. "On top of that, do you think the people of Jacksonville will survive a marriage announcement?"

"I hope so," he said with a grin.

"So it is true? Jake the Rake really is getting married?"

"If she'll have me." Jake, and it seemed the world, waited for April's answer.

Sergeant Sandusky unlocked the cell door. "I can't stand it anymore," he said as April stepped out. "That Phariss fellow was here and cleared you of any wrongdoing. You're free."

"Yes, I am. I'm free of doubt, and I'm free of the past." April searched Jake's face for reassurance that he had forgiven her for being so blind. The smile and loving look he gave her communicated far more than words ever could.

Holding his gaze, she said, "A wise man once told me that everybody needs somebody sometime." Jake opened his arms and April ran joyously into them. In a low voice that only he could hear, she murmured, "I'm happy to be the body he needs."

Their kiss was long and dramatic, and April feared she would end up swooning in front of the crowd. When it was over, a cheer went up among the women in the cell. It spread to the reporters, and to the vice officers, who'd come in to see what all the fuss was about. They didn't know what was going on, but accustomed as they were to cheering their favorite sports hero, their applause was a reflex action.

Molly and Staci danced excitedly around their parents, and April and Jake's embrace enlarged to include them. So much had happened since their first meeting that April could hardly believe Jake was really and truly hers. All she had to do was say yes.

He looked down at her and his eyes were filled with such emotion that the noisy reporters with their questions and flash cameras receded into the never-was. It no longer mattered that a very intimate moment in their lives was not only being observed by over thirty people, but recorded for posterity as well.

As far as April was concerned, there was only one man present, her man. Her Jake. "You tricked me again," she accused him. "But don't worry, this time I was a willing victim."

"Guilty as charged." Jake brushed aside an errant tendril of April's hair and tightened his hold on her. "I think I deserve a life sentence."

The look they exchanged was radiant with their love. "I agree."

The crowd cheered again, and the judge began: "Dearly beloved..."

*"She is not only talented, not only gifted—
LaVyrle Spencer is magic!"*
—Affaire de Coeur

LaVyrle Spencer

LaVyrle Spencer is one of today's best loved authors of bittersweet human drama and captivating romance. And Jove proudly brings you her most unforgettable novels...

____	**YEARS**	0-515-08489-1/$4.95
____	**SEPARATE BEDS**	0-515-09037-9/$4.95
____	**HUMMINGBIRD**	0-515-09160-X/$4.50
____	**A HEART SPEAKS**	0-515-09039-5/$3.95
____	**THE GAMBLE**	0-515-08901-X/$3.95
____	**VOWS**	0-515-09477-3/$4.50
____	**THE HELLION**	0-515-09951-1/$4.50

Please send the titles I've checked above. Mail orders to:
BERKLEY PUBLISHING GROUP
390 Murray Hill Pkwy., Dept. B
East Rutherford, NJ 07073

NAME_____
ADDRESS_____
CITY_____
STATE_____ZIP_____

Please allow 6 weeks for delivery.
Prices are subject to change without notice.

POSTAGE & HANDLING:
$1.00 for one book, $.25 for each additional. Do not exceed $3.50.

BOOK TOTAL $_____
SHIPPING & HANDLING $_____
APPLICABLE SALES TAX $_____
(CA, NJ, NY, PA)
TOTAL AMOUNT DUE $_____
PAYABLE IN US FUNDS.
(No cash orders accepted.)

By the bestselling author of *Savannah*,
To See Your Face Again, and
Before the Darkness Falls

Eugenia Price

The hearts of three families and the soul of a nation torn by the passions of the Civil War.

Stranger in Savannah

Coming in Hardcover May '89

DOUBLEDAY

At All Bookstores

ANNE TYLER

"To read a novel by Anne Tyler is to fall in love!"
—PEOPLE MAGAZINE

Anne Tyler's novels are a rare mixture of laughter and tears. Critics have praised her fine gift for characterization and her skill at blending touching insight and powerful emotions to create superb entertainment.

___	Dinner at the Homesick Restaurant	0-425-09868-0/$4.95
___	The Tin Can Tree	0-425-09903-2/$3.95
___	Morgan's Passing	0-425-09872-9/$3.95
___	Searching for Caleb	0-425-09876-1/$3.95
___	If Morning Ever Comes	0-425-09883-4/$3.95
___	The Clock Winder	0-425-09902-4/$3.95
___	A Slipping-Down Life	0-425-10362-5/$3.95
___	Celestial Navigation	0-425-09840-0/$3.95
___	Earthly Possessions	0-425-10167-3/$3.95
___	The Accidental Tourist	0-425-09291-7/$4.95

Please send the titles I've checked above. Mail orders to:
BERKLEY PUBLISHING GROUP
390 Murray Hill Pkwy., Dept. B
East Rutherford, NJ 07073

NAME_____
ADDRESS_____
CITY_____
STATE_____ ZIP_____

Please allow 6 weeks for delivery.
Prices are subject to change without notice.

POSTAGE & HANDLING:
$1.00 for one book, $.25 for each additional. Do not exceed $3.50.

BOOK TOTAL $_____
SHIPPING & HANDLING $_____
APPLICABLE SALES TAX $_____
(CA, NJ, NY, PA)
TOTAL AMOUNT DUE $_____
PAYABLE IN US FUNDS.
(No cash orders accepted.)

Look for the Berkley Paperback Bestseller!

"A compelling tale of a family torn asunder... brilliant...heart-rending."
—*Chicago Tribune*

THE STUNNING NATIONAL BESTSELLER
When it comes to love, we are all...

AT RISK
ALICE HOFFMAN

Every now and then, a novel comes along that captures the hearts of its readers in a way that is utterly unforgettable. *Ordinary People, Terms of Endearment, The Good Mother*—and now, Alice Hoffman's *At Risk*...

A small town. An ordinary American home. The abiding power of love. All come into play in this affecting novel of a family challenged by a tragedy—until a charming, courageous girl shows them how to embrace life...on any terms.

On sale in September wherever paperbacks are sold.